LIFE AFTER THE GHETTO

Copyright © 2016 Renita Towns
Published by Red Bud Ave Publications, LLC

Sale of this book without a front cover may be unauthorized. If this book is without a cover, it may have been reported to the publisher as *unsold or destroyed* and neither author nor the publisher may have received payment for it.

All rights reserved. No part of this book may be reproduced, stored in or introduced into a retrieval system, or transmitted, in any form or by any means electronic, mechanical, photocopying, recording or otherwise, without prior written permission of both the copyright owner and the publisher of this book.

Publisher's Note:

This is a work of fiction. Any names to historical events, real people, living and dead, or to real locales are intended only to give the fiction a setting in historic reality. Other names, characters, places, business and incidents are either the product of the author's imagination or are used fictitiously, and their resemblance, if any, to real life counterparts is entirely coincidental.

Library of Congress Catalog No.: Pending

ISBN 10: 0-9844397-2-2
ISBN 13: 978-0-9844397-2-0
Cover Design: Robert Ford, Jr.
Editor: Jon B. King

FIRST EDITION

Printed in the United States of America

Red Bud Ave Publications, LLC

Red Bud Ave Publications, LLC is the avenue to that puts your voice in print. Red Bud Ave Publications, LLC is a subsidy publishing company located in St. Louis, MO. Our purpose is to offer those who want to publish their work the assistance in which they will need to get published. Red Bud Ave Publications, LLC serves as the author's professional resource to the author's publishing needs. Please visit www.redbudave.com for more information.

CHECK OUT OTHER TITLES BY RED BUD AVE PUBLICATIONS

TAYLOR MADE
SIMPLY TAYLOR MADE
WASHED UP
TALES FROM THE LOU
DIAMONDS ARE TRULY FOREVER
MISPLACED LOYALTY

Dedication

This book is dedicated to Quintin "Hershey" Goodwin, Jr.

Hershey, it's going to be some good days and there are going to be some bad ones. The good will outweigh the bad! Hershey, never think that your dad left you, he just stepped back so you can show him that you can be the man that he instilled in you! But never walk around sad and blue because you make him feel like you mad with him. If you wake up feeling down, go do something your dad taught you. Not only will you feel better, but when you open your front door and the window to your heart, the sun will be shining letting you know that your daddy, Mr. Quintin Goodwin, Sr. is dancing and hollering saying, "He's twice the man that I raised him to be!"

CHAPTER 1

It was a very cold day in St. Louis. Peggy sat on the floor looking at Lucy thinking about what they were about to get into before the day came to an end. Then the phone rang interrupting their thoughts. As Peggy answered the phone she could hear someone crying on the other end of the phone. While holding the phone, she was wondering who it was and why they felt the need to call her. Then she heard a familiar voice whimpering and whispering her name. Peggy became anxious and couldn't take it any longer. She decided to break the silence because she grew with curiosity trying to figure out who was on my phone crying and why they called her.

"Hello, this is Peggy, who is this?" she said slightly agitated.

There was still just a low humming sound of crying and words trying to escape from the mouth of the stranger who was on the other end of the phone.

As she tried to make out the voice, she realized it was her best friend Ann.

"What's wrong, Ann? Why are you crying?" she asked.

"I was up on Mimika walking to the store." Ann said and stopped in mid-sentence, still crying.

"So you're crying because you were walking to the store?" Peggy asked.

"No, I was walking to the store when I saw Baby D with some other girl." Ann said.

"Why are you walking instead of driving your car?" Peggy asked Ann.

Ann began to tell Peggy about how she let Baby D use her car.

"When I saw them, and told them to get out of the car, Baby D got out and started hitting and kicking me. He called me all kinds of ugly bitches and dick suckers. So, I ran to the passenger side and told that bitch to get out of my car. Baby D told her to get out and kick my ass. She got out the car and I rushed her. That bitch ass nigga helped her, he pulled me up off her and they stated jumping me! They took my car, too. My God, Peggy, what am I going to do, I straight love this nigga." Ann continued to cry as she gave details about the incident.

"Ann calm down. So what's the girl name?" Peggy asked not being really sure if she believed Ann.

"April." Ann replied.

"How long has this being going on?" Peggy asked.

"About seven months." Ann said.

"Damn! You just now telling me? You've been going through this shit alone? Well the first thing we are going to do, is get your car back. Tonight we are going to have a drink and we will put together a plan for Baby D and this April bitch. Ann, you have to be sure that you are done fucking with him because if you aren't, I can't help you. So tell me what the deal is, Ann!"

"Peggy, girl I won't ever mess with him again." Ann answered not being really sure and confident in her response. The only thing she was sure of was that, she knew that's what Peggy wanted to hear.

"Okay then, let the games begin." Peggy responded not sure how far she should go being that Ann hadn't really convinced her that the relationship between her and Baby D was really over.

Ann, so curious to know the plan, asked Peggy what they were going to do.

Peggy quickly responded, "We are going to show this bitch ass nigga why they call Mimika Avenue murdaville. Be ready at 8:30 tonight. Dress fly!"

"Peggy where are we going?" Lucy looked up after ear hustling for about fifteen minutes.

Peggy looked at Lucy almost forgetting she was even in her presence, "Well since you must know, we're just going out to Laclede's Landing to put this plan together."

Peggy got off the phone and started to think about the plan she was about to put in place.

Lucy was already dressed. She was the type that stayed ready just so she wouldn't have to worry about getting ready. Peggy was so last minute but she was glad Lucy was there. All she had to do was shower and put on her clothes. Lucy hustle was hair. Every time she went to work on someone's head all she would do is slay. She was Peggy's personal stylist.

Peggy hopped in the shower. Once out the shower, she put on a pair of Seven Jeans with a Seven shirt to match. She put on some powder blue stilettos with the belt and purse to match her shirt. She sat down and let Lucy style her hair. When she was done she grabbed her chrome 357 and her car keys. She and Lucy were headed out the door.

She hopped on the highway headed to the city. As she and Lucy were getting off Highway 40 onto I-170 north. They saw a car that looked just like Ann's. She grabbed her cell phone and dialed Ann.

"Girl, what's up?" Ann answered quickly as Peggy's name flashed across the screen.

"I'm on the highway. Does your license plate say LAM 777?" Peggy asked as she eyed Ann's car.

Ann replied, "Yeah!"

"I'm on 70 behind your car now but, Baby D isn't driving, a girl is!" That's when Peggy figured that the girl she was looking at had to be April. She put on her blinker to get on the side of the car so she could get a good look at the driver's face.

Peggy noticed the driver immediately. Unless, this was another chic from earlier, April was not April. Peggy was looking at an old friend from grade school name Tara.

Peggy laughed and looked at Lucy, "I went to school with that bitch. So, that's the hoe Baby D fucking around with."

Lucy looked at the driver and back at Peggy, "Bitch, you play too much. Ain't that your daddy's daughter?"

Peggy became very puzzled. She knew her sister was a bit trigger happy when it came to beef. She tried to figure out had Ann ever been around her dad's people.

Peggy looked at Lucy, "Ann said the girl name was April. I know if it was Tara with Baby D, she would have shot Ann. She would've left her for dead, flat right there. So, I gotta find out what's going on. Therefore, when Tara gets off the highway, I'll get off behind her."

Lucy looked at Peggy, "This don't look like this going to end well for Ann."

Peggy's mind became overwhelmed with crazy thoughts. She sat silently as she continue to follow her sister.

Peggy noticed that Tara was about to exit at Goodfellow. She was right behind her. She followed slowly behind her so she went notice that she was close on her tail.

When Peggy unnoticed that Tara was headed on Emma she began blowing her horn to get her attention. Tara pulled over and

Peggy exited the car. As she walked towards Tara and got closer to her car door, Peggy could see Tara picking up her nine millimeter.

Tara noticed it was Peggy, sat her nine back down and opened the car door.

"What's up lil sis?" Peggy said to her.

Tara looked up and said, "You were getting ready to be a dead bitch!"

They both stated laughing, and Peggy told her, "You gotta find yours, mines out and ready. Don't forget I'm J. J.'s daughter, too. So, girl who car is this you driving?"

Tara said, "This piece of shit!" I got it from this girl named, April. She sold it to me for twenty-five hundred dollars."

"Why? You already have a '07 Range Rover and living in five hundred thousand dollar house. You don't even need this car!" Peggy was confused.

"Yeah, I know. But why are you asking about my car?" Tara wanted to end the small talk. Sister or not she didn't need to know all her business.

"Because Tara, this is my friend Ann's car. Her ex-boyfriend, Baby D and April beat her down and took her car! But now you telling me April sold you the car?" Peggy questioned.

"Yes, sista! You mean to tell me that this hoe done got my money and this motha-fucking car not even hers to sell. This bitch is dead!" Tara became easily frustrated thinking about the hassle she may have to go through.

"Chill out Tara. I got a plan for this bitch and Baby D. I'm about to go get my nails done, meet me at my house at 7:30 p.m. I will be going over my plan then."

"This better be good, because I can just go and kill this bitch!" Tara rolled her eyes.

"We gonna kill both of them, but we going to get rich in the process. Better yet we're gonna get rich first!" Peggy stated.

"Alright big sis, I'll see you tonight." Tara said without a care in the world.

"I'm just curious and if you don't mind me asking, Tara, what exactly are you gonna do with Ann's car?" Peggy waited on an answer.

"That bitch can pay me for it she wants the motha-fucka back!" Tara had a serious look on her face.

"I'll talk to you about that tonight." Peggy began to walk to get back to her car.

"You don't have shit to say about me and this car, if it ain't about money. The dumb whore is yo friend, not mines!" Tara yelled as Peggy walked away.

"Well that makes two dumb whores, because you out of your twenty-five hundred dollars. Dress sexy tonight, we going to fuck with some rich white boys." Peggy laughed as she walked back to get in the car with Lucy.

"I always dress sexy bitch!" Tara yelled.

While Peggy was getting her nails done, it came to her how too really get up on Baby D. Ann didn't know how much money the nigga had but she did.

"Lucy, we gotta go and pick up Ann now. She can get ready over my house. Let me call her."

Lucy was not much of a talker but Peggy knew she was down for whatever when it came to her. Peggy dialed Ann. She answered immediately already knowing it was Peggy.

"What's up girl?" Ann was sitting waiting on this call.

"Hey, Ann, what's up girl?" Peggy didn't wait on her to respond, "Check this out, I'm going to pick you up now so you can get ready at my house. I'm coming down Park Lane now so come on out."

Ann came right outside and hopped in the car with Lucy and Peggy. As soon as she closed the door. A cell phone began to ring. Everybody checked their cell phone. It was Peggy's phone ringing.

"What's up baby?" Red asked when he heard Peggy's voice.

A big smile came across Peggy's face as she was gathering her thoughts to answer her man's question, "Nothing just picking up Ann. What's up with you, getting rich?"

Red liked to hear questions about getting rich. He smiled when Peggy asked him what time was. He immediately responded, "Time to show these pussy as niggas that there is life after the ghetto!"

Peggy loved to hear him talk about life after the ghetto. Now she wanted to see him.

"Are you on Mimika?" Peggy asked.

"Oh, baby yeah." Red smiled

"Well I guess I have to come on the block and see my man. Since you haven't been home in four days. I am on Park Lane. I just picked up Ann. I'll be there in about ten minutes." Peggy to Red.

Peggy sped across town. Since Red hadn't been home in four days she said she wasn't going to sweat him. She was just going to wait on him to call her. As soon as she got the call she was racing across town to go see her man.

Peggy made it on Mimika in ten minutes flat. She ran every light and bumped the stop signs. The car was quiet the entire time. Lucy and Ann knew not to question Peggy's driving.

Peggy turned on Mimika Avenue. She started talking as though she was talking to herself, "Girl it's colder than a mothafucka out here. But Mimika popping like it's the summer time. Who are all these bitches out here on the block? These hoes are just popping up around here, fucking other people's men and sucking dicks and everything. Speaking of fucking, good thing my family still own that house! My pussy been jumping for four days! And it's time to stop!"

"So, what the fuck does that mean?" Lucy asked a tad bit confused and startled from the drive.

"Bitch that mean Red needs to fuck my brains out in that house. Shit, where the fuck is Red? I just told him I was on my way up here." Peggy grew with frustration.

"There your man is." Lucy pointed as she seen Red standing on a lot where a home once stood.

"Who is this bitch up in Red's face?" Peggy hurried to find a parking spaced.

"Hell if I know, you know bitches pop up around here like crazy." Ann said.

"Lucy and Ann, I'll be right back." Peggy hurried out the car.

"Peggy, I know damn well you don't think Lucy and I about to sit out here in this could while you trying to go fuck?" Ann said.

"Ann, I need a quick nut, it's lonely. It's gonna take about an hour, but y'all can come in and keep warm. Here Ann, take these keys because I got to find out who this bitch is all up in my man's face." Peggy tossed the keys to Ann and shut the door.

As Peggy was getting out of her car, she grabbed her purse to take it with her. Walking to the corner of Schulte and Mimika, Red back was to her, she grabbed him for the back and spun him around. She then threw her tongue in his mouth and started rubbing on his dick and looking at the unknown girl at the same time.

When Peggy let him go, the girl asked, "Who the fuck are you?"

Peggy said, "I'm the crazy bitch that's getting ready to blow your fucking brains out! Whore, if you don't carry your Payless shoe wearing ass down the street, and stay the fuck out of his face."

Red turned around and said, "This is Honey. One of my workers. She's the one holding down Era for me."

"Well, Honey let me holler at you for a minute." Peggy said.

Honey was cool and played her position. Red walked away. As he walked away Peggy let him know to meet her in the house in about two minutes. When he was out of sight, Peggy eyes were back on Honey.

"Well now we can talk. I'm gonna talk and you listen. Next time I see you up in my man's face, I'm going to kick your ass bitch. You work Era, not my man, do I make myself clear? Honey I'm going to let you slide this time, don't let this happen again!" Peggy felt like she had laid the law down.

"Ann, where the fuck did Red leave to?" Lucy asked trying to watch what was all going on out there on the block.

Ann answered telling Lucy that Red went into the house. They both watch Peggy as she went into the house that Red had just entered. When Peggy got on the porch she shot twice in the air.

Red damn near pissed his pants. "Peggy, what's wrong with you girl?"

"Negro, let me tell you something, if I ever see that bitch in your face again, I'm gonna put your ass to sleep do you understand me?"

"Peggy that girls works for me!" Red said.

"Well tell the trick to work Era and keep her ass off Mimika. Is that why you haven't been home in four days?"

"Girl, I been out here making money."

"I stopped by so I could bust a nut and get sucked on by my man, but fuck it now." Peggy turned to leave.

"Peggy come here baby." Red grabbed her arm as she turned to walk out the door.

"No, you better have your ass at home tonight." Peggy looked at Red waiting for a reaction.

Ann could no longer see Peggy standing in the door. She told Lucy to watch out as she went to see what was going on with Red and Peggy.

When she made it up on the porch she noticed that the door was cracked. She pushed the door opened not going all the way in making sure Lucy could see her, "Red, who is that dude sitting in your car? Ann asked.

"That's my brother, JaDarrell." Red said proudly.

"Hook me up, bro!" Ann smiled.

"Girl, we ain't got time for your bullshit, plus you got Baby D. That nigga come here talking that shit to my brother, we will be shooting at each other, fuck that!" Red waved his hand in the air.

"Red, I don't fuck with Baby D no more. Here, take my phone number and give it to him. Alright?" Ann waited to give him the number.

Peggy laughed, "Red, I will see you at home tonight."

Ann and Peggy turned to leave out the house. Peggy walked right over to Red's car. JaDarrell opened the door as they approached the car.

"Hey JaDarrell, what's up man? Somebody wants to meet you." Peggy smiled.

"What's up sis-in-law, how you doing?" JaDarrell returned the smile.

"I'm fine. Hey boo, this my friend Ann, she want to holla at you." Peggy cut the small talk.

"What's up baby, I'm JaDarrell."

"I'm Ann. Red got my number give me a call sometime."

"How about Sunday?" JaDarrell inquired.

"That's cool." Ann replied.

Red walked down to the car to see what was going on.

"Let's ride Ann. Later baby, don't be late getting home so I can ride that dick. Ann what time is it?" Peggy asked.

"Time for you to tell me the plan?" Ann wanted to know how they were going to set up Baby D.

Peggy began to pull out of the parking space, "Well, first I need to tell you that Tara got your car. She bought it from April."

"Your sister, Tara?" Ann asked.

Lucy chuckled and looked back to see Ann's face expression.

"Yeah. Tara gonna help us take care of Baby D and April. She gonna meet us at my house." Peggy's cell phone rang and she looked at the screen, "Shit, there she is now. Hello Tara."

"What's up Trick? I'm letting you know now I am not giving you shit, so don't think you getting my car!" Tara laughed.

"Stop, Tara." Peggy said.

"Stop shit, that's your friend. I don't give a damn about her dumb ass. She can buy this mothafucka back." Tara continued to laugh but she was dead serious.

"I'm not buying shit back," said Ann, "you got me fucked up."

"I got you fucked up bitch. I'll come through this phone and fuck you up, open your mouth one more time."

"Calm down Tara and Ann! We need to get started on our plan." Peggy said.

"What's the plan, Peggy?" Lucy asked. She didn't like how this situation was even starting.

Peggy decided to let them all in on what she had going on in her head. She looked at the phone to make sure Tara was still there. When she notice that she was still on the phone she began to talk, "I am going to have Kezia and her friend Pam to come down here and have them to help us set Baby D up. It's been a minute since Kezia been here so I know people, especially Baby D doesn't know that we are related. So this going go cool. We can put Kezia on Baby D and he won't have a clue. Tara, call Kezia and tell her our plan and see if she is down. And tell her we need Pam, too. Let them know this job pays top dollars!"

Tara got off the phone and called Kezia.

Kezia didn't ask one question. She knew her family wouldn't have called if they didn't need her. She called Peggy to let her know she was down for the cause. Kezia decided to call Peggy to find out the details.

Peggy pressed answer as soon as she saw Kezia's name scroll across the screen.

"Hey sis, I need you and Pam here like yesterday!" Peggy laughed.

Kezia was all in, "Peggy, Pam and I are down. We just don't have a way to get there.

Peggy shook her head, "Look up the flights and call me back with the info and I'll take care of it on this end. All you will have to do is get to the airport."

Kezia agreed and let her know she would call her back with the details. Peggy told her to let her know their arrival time and they ended the call.

Peggy called Tara back and let her know that Kezia and Pam where on their way. Before they got off the phone she let her know they would all go over the plan when everyone was there. She didn't want them to know she was still thinking about the set up. She just knew she was about to break Baby D down.

Tara was sitting in front of Peggy's house waiting on her to arrive.

The four ladies walked into Peggy's house. Before they could get comfortable Red walked through the door. Peggy gave Ann the keys to her Lexus so she and Lucy could get home. They all were about to walk out the door.

Before they could make it out the door, Red asked with a serious look on his face, "What the fuck you doing in my motha fucking house?"

"Calm down baby, what's the problem?" Peggy was caught off guard.

"Why is she in my house?" Reggie pointed at Tara.

"Red, Tara is my sister." Peggy answered trying to read Red's face expression.

"What you mean that's your sister?" Red said trying to figure out what was taking place.

Peggy nervously responded, "Red, we have the same daddy."

"That's right brother-in-law!" Tara said with a smirk on her face.

"Sis, I didn't know this was the Red that you were with. I still say you so damn black, that's why they need to call you, Blue!" Tara was being sarcastic as she watched Red's anger grow.

"Fuck you girl!" Red wanted to end her life right there but he had too many witnesses in the room.

Red was real dark with pretty white teeth, blue eyes and bow-legs. Dressed his ass off and the nigga always smelled good, too! That was just the few things that attracted Peggy to him.

"See you big sis, alright?" Tara knew it was best for her to leave. She and Red didn't have the best relationship to be in the same room.

"So Red, how long have you known, Tara?" Peggy asked.

"Baby, I didn't know she was your sister?" Red said slightly irritated.

"I know you're not telling me that you fucked my sister!" Peggy insinuated.

"Hell naw, but your sister is the one that shot me five years ago." Red said as he continued to show his irritation.

"Yeah, my sister doesn't take any shit." Peggy chuckled not really caring why Tara pulled the trigger. She just wanted Red to fill up her insides and that's all that mattered.

"I know that now. So Peggy, what are you up to?" Red asked knowing it wasn't a good time to discuss what he had instore for Tara later on down the line.

"Nothing we're just kicking it because our lil sister will be here in the morning."

Peggy was ready to end the small talk, "All shit! Peggy wants to make love to her man!"

Peggy followed Red to the bedroom. As soon as she got into the room she pulled Red over to the bed and started kissing him and sucking on his bottom lip. That bottom lip action turned him on. Red started kissing her on her neck, moving down to her nipples, making her as hot as he pulled off her shirt. Peggy laid back on the bed and let him undress her. He started kissing her inner thighs, and put two of his fingers in her pussy.

"Ooh Re, baby that feels so good." Peggy screamed out.

He took his fingers out of her pussy and started sucking on them.

"Baby this shit taste good!" Red said seductively.

"Make love to me baby." Peggy demanded as she began to take off his pants and all she could think about to herself is how much she loved Red. As his boxers came down, her pussy got hotter and wetter. As he put all twelve inches inside of her, making Peggy cum over and over. He wanted to try something different with Peggy. He tied her left leg to the bed post and her right hand to the opposite post.

When he had her like he wanted her he said, "I want to fuck now!"

"Deeper baby!" Peggy screamed, "Ooh shit this feel so good!"

"Peggy, you feel so damn good!" Red said.

"I know C. B. P. is always good." Peggy chuckled.

"What the fuck is C. B. P.?" Red asked with a look of confusion.

"It's something I was born with." Peggy spoke with confidence.

"What the fuck is it?" Red was quite tired of the game.

"C. B. P. is just that come back pussy. Everybody doesn't have it." Peggy said proudly.

"But, you do?" Red chuckled.

"You tell me, you always jump in it." Peggy was waiting on Red to agree with her.

"Damn baby, the shit so good I guess you do have it!" Red felt the need to stroke her ego.

"I know!" Peggy said with her hands on her hips.

The sex had come to an end and Peggy was ready to cuddle. She lay her head on Red's chest and played in his chest hairs with her the tips of her fingers.

"I believe we are gonna have a bad ass winter." Peggy said to Red.

"Why do you say that?" Red inquired.

"I believe that things are going to move slowly and the crime will be on the rise. Remember what we dreamt about? Now is the time to live the life. I think I'm going to quit this job with in next six weeks. We can just go somewhere warm." Peggy began to think of a warmer climate.

Red understood what she was trying to say and he was ready for a change. He just wasn't ready like Peggy was.

"So, do you think in the morning I can just tell the maid to help me pack? I think we can just move to Florida in the next six weeks. I thinks it's time to show people on Mimika there is life after the ghetto. Baby we have over 12 million dollars, the drug game has been good to us. But, it's time to get out while we're still ahead." Peggy tried to convince Red it was time to leave.

"Baby, I think it's going to be a crazy winter. But, six weeks is not enough time to prepare this type of transition. We need to aim for at least six months and if things go faster we can leave earlier than that." Red tried to buy himself some time before he actually made the move to Florida.

After talking, Peggy fell asleep in Red's arm. A few hours into her sleep Peggy could hear her cell phone ringing.

"Peggy, answer the phone!" Tara yelled at her phone.

Peggy turned over and grabbed her phone from the nightstand. "Hello."

"What's up sis? Are you up?" Tara asked.

"What time is it?" Peggy asked.

"It's 10:45." Tara said.

"Shit! Let me hop in the shower and get ready. Kezia's plane lands at 11:45." Peggy gasped.

As Peggy was coming out of the bathroom, Red asked what time it was, "11 in the morning." Peggy said.

"Damn!" Red spoke loudly. "Baby I got to meet JaDarrell on Schulte."

Red jumped in the shower, got dressed and left. Five minutes later Tara and Ann were at the door.

"Come in and let's get down to biz!" Peggy said as she let Tara and Ann in the door.

"Damn! Where's your maid? I'm ready to eat!" Tara shouted.

"She's cooking bitch, now let's talk biz." Peggy said to Tara.

Mrs. Brown entered the dinner room with breakfast.

Peggy turned and looked in her maid's direction, "Mrs. Brown, you can just set the food up. We can serve ourselves. Oh and Mrs. Brown, can you pack up all my summer clothes and shoes and Mr. Strong's things, too."

Mrs. Brown was from off Mimika. At an early age she had been diagnosed as bipolar with autism. She had a hard to time keeping employment. One summer Peggy was driving down Mimika and Mrs. Brown's landlord was sitting her things out on the curb. Peggy stopped found out how much she owed. She paid the landlord and gave Mrs. Brown a job.

"Peggy, why are you packing up your clothes?" Mrs. Brown asked.

"Because summer is over. That's all Mrs. Brown." Peggy answered.

Ann was getting tired of the bonding session Peggy was having with the maid, "Now let's hear this plan." Ann said.

"First thing I need one of you to do is go and get Pam and Kezia a cell phone, and get both of them a hotel suite on different floors. Then one of you get on the phone and rent both of them a car. I don't want anybody knowing that we know them." Peggy gave out the instructions.

"Alright, I'll go and call the hotel." Ann said.

Ann talk with Peggy for a few seconds. She let her know that Lucy had taken care of the rental cars with her little hook-up at Avis car rental. She continued to let her know that Lucy little brother would be at the airport to pick the girls up. Lucy little brother Larry was not in the streets and barely even came outside. So, if anyone just so happened to be at the airport when Kezia and Pam arrived they wouldn't be able to trace it back to Peggy. Ann ended her call with Lucy.

Ann looked over at Peggy trying to read her thoughts. She was thinking so hard that wrinkles formed in her forehead. Peggy noticed Ann just standing there and looked up at her, "What's up with you, Ann?"

Ann answered quickly, "The girls should be here in about thirty minutes."

"Alright, when they get here, we'll go over our plan." Peggy said.

"I hope you got this shit mapped out." Ann said.

"I do. When we get through with Baby D, that nigga gonna wish he never came on Mimika. Ann, while we are waiting on everybody, you can go and get their cell phones." Peggy turned towards her sister, "Tara, while Ann is gone I need to talk to you."

"About what?" Tara asked.

"Tara, if this shit goes like I planned, we'll become rich as hell. And you will have to leave St. Louis." Peggy informed her.

"Damn Peggy, you act like we're talking about millions!" Tara snapped.

"I am. Ann doesn't know the kind of money this nigga is working with, but I do. And I'm sure that bitch April do, too." Peggy said.

"Is that why you packing your clothes." Tara asked.

"That's right." Peggy said.

"So, where you going, Ohio?" Tara asked, trying to think of her next move.

"Tara, I need you find out where you going and buy a house there." Peggy was hoping Tara would take heed to what she was suggesting to her.

"Peggy, I just put a $100,000 down on a house in Vegas. Don't anybody know about this except me and now you." Tara said in a sarcastic tone letting her know she not the only one that already had a plan.

Peggy could hear music so she walked over to the window and looked out. When she seen Kezia exit the car she smiled. Kezia and Peggy slightly resembled each other. Kezia was about twenty-five pounds lighter than Peggy, minus the mole on her cheek. If they both possessed the caramel bronze skin tone they probably wouldn't be able to pull it off. Being that Peggy was a shade darker with short pixie haircut and Kezia wore the long Brazilian weave it kind of through off their similarities.

"Here come my motha fucking sister now. Let them in." Peggy was so excited.

"Hey sis, how you been doing?" Kezia said as she entered the door.

Everyone said their hellos and they all embraced each other. Kezia stepped back to take a look at Peggy's house.

Kezia looked towards Peggy, "I see you, look at this house! Fuck all the talking about I want to be like Mike, I want to be like you bitch!"

Everybody started laughing.

Peggy looked Pam up and down. Pam had the perfect physique. She was thicker than a snicker in all the right places. Shorty was a ten. She and K. Michelle could pass for sisters.

Peggy spoke softly across the room, "Pam you are perfect, did Kezia fill you in on what we want?"

"Yeah, I'm in." Pam agreed.

"Alright then, let's get down to biz. Kezia and Pam, you can't let no one know that we're sisters. When you see us in the club or in the streets you and Pam got to act like you don't know us. Now, let's talk. Pam, you're going to get to know Ann's ex-boyfriend, his name is Baby D. You got make this nigga fall in love with you." Peggy gave her instructions to her family.

"Alright, Ann, fill us in on what this nigga like and what he don't like." Kezia was intrigued.

"Pam, make this nigga tell you all his secrets. He doesn't like girls that get high. He doesn't like big mouth girls. And when he and his boys are taking, walk away. That makes him think he's the shit. And he loves for a woman to tell him how good he looks and how good he smells. And when you are having sex with him, always call his name and tell him how good it is. When you sucking his dick," Ann was letting them know how to get close to Baby D.

"Wait a minute, I'm not sucking his dick, fuck that!" Pam yelled cutting Ann off.

"Pam, we're talking about Big Money if our plan works out, you can go back home with about $350,000." Peggy intervened.

The sound of money changed Pam's mind. She quickly responded, "All shit!!!! Well say, that's ight for that kind of money; I'll suck his daddy's dick."

"I know that's right!" Tara said.

Ann continued, "Like I was saying, when sucking his dick, play with his nuts at the same time, it drives him crazy!"

Peggy waited on Ann to finish before she chimed in, "Now Tara I need you to find out where the party is as so I can have Pam and Kezia there. Kezia, you are going to get with Baby D's right hand man. His name is Joe. He doesn't talk much and he loves caramel toned girls. Not too bright and not too dark."

"Peggy, do Baby D and April know that you and Tara are sisters?" Kezia asked.

Peggy began to answer her sister's question, "Hell my man just found out last night. Daddy always said, never tell who your family is because that gives nigga a jump on you and your family if they are looking for you." Peggy turned towards Tara, "Tara, I need you to get Pam and Kezia small gun and keep it with you at all times."

"Big sis, I don't fuck with small guns. Tara, get me a 44, I don't shoot to play. When I shoot a motha-fucker, I shoot to kill." Kezia had to let Peggy know what the deal was.

"I heard that." Peggy laughed as she watched her maid enter the room.

"Mrs. Peggy." Ms. Brown had gotten Peggy's attention.

"Yes, Ms. Brown?" Peggy answered.

"I think you should turn on the TV. It's something on the news that I think you would want to see." Ms. Brown informed Peggy.

Tara wanted to know what was on the news. She anxiously said, "Turned on the television on Channel 2, they got the best news."

They all sat silently watching as the reporter stood on the corner of Mimika give her report as she stood in front of the crime scene. The headline that scrolled across the screen read *Suspects Shot Are Expected To Be Okay.*

Peggy heart dropped. Knowing that news never gave accurate reports in the beginning, "Give me the phone so I can call

Red." Peggy stomped her foot on the floor as she waited on Red to answer his phone, "Red, hurry, come on Red, baby answer the phone."

Peggy hung up each time the voicemail came on. She had called his phone six times. On her seventh try he finally answered.

"Yeah!" Red answered.

"Baby, what the fuck is going on?" Peggy asked.

"Nothing baby," said Red. "I'm cool."

"Bullshit, the shit is on the news. So what the fuck happened?" Peggy needed to know what was going on. She was content from hearing his voice but she needed to know what was going on in the neighborhood that made them their money.

Red really didn't want to talk on the phone but he knew she wasn't just gonna settle for what he was telling her, "Those bitch ass niggas, Pete and Dave come shooting at JaDarrell about that bitch Tracey he used to fuck with."

"That's fucked up, is JaDarrell ok?" Peggy asked.

"Yeah." Red responded.

Peggy had more questions, "Was Tracey with them?"

Red answered nonchalantly, "Yeah. That's who pointed us out."

"Did anybody get hit?" Peggy asked as the girls watched every word that rolled off her tongue.

"Yeah, I got hit in the arm but I'm cool, I'll be home later tonight, we'll talk alright?" Red ended the call.

Peggy was fine with hearing his voice. She didn't get an attitude about the way he ended the call. She knew he wasn't going to do much talking over the phone. The sound of his voice put her at ease.

"What the fuck is going on?" said Ann.

Peggy knew they all were anxious to know what was going on. She didn't let them wait long before she went on to tell them what was going on, "Pete and Dave went over there shooting at JaDarrell about that bitch Tracey and Red got hit in the arm. And check this out, the bitch was with them."

"So what's up? We're getting ready to kill this whore and Dave," Ann said. "We gonna do this shit tonight!"

Peggy looked in Ann's direction, "Now Ann, you still cool with Tracey right?"

"Hell naw, the bitch just tried to kill my brother-in-law!" Ann barked.

"Don't worry about that, this bitch will know in the next life not to fuck with me." Peggy said.

"Peggy, she's not going to deal with Ann now!" Kezia said.

Pam asked, "Why not? Doesn't she know you all are friends?"

Kezia chimed in, "The bitch doesn't know you all are friends?"

Ann answered their question, "The bitch doesn't know shit about us."

"Ann, call that bitch Tracey. I can get next to Dave with just one phone call." Peggy said. She was upset that someone had just tried to take her man's life.

"You can?" Ann asked wanting to know how Peggy was about to make that happen. She knew Peggy knew the right people but that usually came through Red. She wondered how she was about to get this done without Red giving her the required information she needed.

"Call this nigga Dave and make him think you're going fuck him. Well, I'm going fuck him, just not the way he's thinking! Call him, call now!" Peggy instructed Tara.

"Yeah, hi daddy." Tara said to Dave on the phone.

"Who is this?" Dave asked not knowing who was on the other end of his phone.

"Tara." She said.

"What's up, baby?" Dave said knowing exactly what Tara was on his other end.

"You baby." Tara said sounding too hip.

"How are you doing?" Dave dick got hard instantly hearing her voice as he reminisced on their previous sex escapades.

"Not too good." Tara was about to pour it on thick.

"Why?" Dave knew what she wanted but he wanted her to say it to him.

"Because today is my birthday and I want some of daddy's dick." Tara lied, "Daddy, can you help me with this problem?"

"Baby, that's not a problem." Dave was ready for the sweet pussy that stayed wet. He didn't care if it was her birthday or not.

"Well, can I come ride that dick?" Tara asked.

"For sho, but you know we got to keep this shit on the low." Dave insisted.

Tara got offended. "You the one telling your boys everything."

"Never that. Where are you? I have to meet you at the hotel." Dave was done with the small talk. He wanted to fuck.

"Which one?" Tara asked.

"The Marriot at the airport." Dave gave her the location.

Tara had to think about that. Everyone in St. Louis frequent that spot. She even saw folks fucking on the parking lot of that hotel, "Everybody goes there, somebody will see us there."

"No, they won't, I already have a room there, room 3224." Dave had already had the room reserved and booked for two weeks.

Tara agreed, "Alright, daddy? I'll see you in thirty minutes."

Dave was ready and headed in the direction as he was already in his car, "All right sexy."

"Ann, call Tracey." Peggy said.

"I just did. We're going to the Loft tonight. I'm meeting her there at 10:30 pm." Ann was already on it.

"Cool, and that bitch will be dead before 11:30, but Dave first." Peggy said to her crew.

"Kezia and Pam that's the hotel you'll be staying in, so you all can leave with Tara. When you all get there call me with your room numbers. Tara, you find his room key, Pam will be hanging outside his door, give her the key so we can get in. Make sure that you play the music really loud so he won't hear us come in and make sure he cannot get to his gun. Go take care of this biz, give me a call in twenty-five minutes alright." Peggy said.

"We out here!" Tara said as she exited the house going to meet Dave.

Peggy was ready to go, she was out the door before everyone was out of her house, "Lock the door, Ann."

Ann looked at how fast Peggy was moving. Red getting shot must have thrown her off. She wasn't really thinking and Ann could see it. She stopped Peggy and said, "Peggy, give me some tennis shoes, get a pair of the Nike's and throw me one of the blue one's."

Peggy almost forgot her cellphone, "All shit, give my cell phone to me."

Peggy knew she wasn't thinking. She asked Ann to give her few minutes. She tried to gather her thoughts. She sat on the steps that lead to the second floor of her us. Her thoughts were interrupted with the ringing of her cellphone.

"Hello. What's up?" Peggy asked when she seen Kezia name come across the screen.

Pam called here with the information and let her know she need to get something to write down what she was about to tell her.

Peggy called out to Ann, "Ann, write this room down, Pam room is 5069 and Kezia room number is 6038. We'll meet in room after everything's over with. Is Kezia down there by Dave's door waiting on Tara to give her the key?"

"Here she comes now." Pam said.

"Does she have the key?" Peggy asked.

"She got it." Pam replied.

"We'll meet you in Pam's room in fifteen minutes alright? Ann, get two pantsuits out and some shoes and my handbag so we can change clothes before we leave the hotel. You know Baby D and the other nigga will be at the Loft tonight. What time would he be getting here?" Peggy was trying to think as she talked on the phone.

"About midnight." Pam said.

Ann and Peggy hopped in her car. Peggy didn't even let the car warm up before she pulled off. Ten minutes on the road and they weren't far from their destination the way Peggy was driving.

"Slow down Peggy before we flagged!" Ann yelled not sure how Peggy was going to react. She didn't like anyone telling her how to drive.

"Shit, we here now." Peggy said as she was about to get off at her exit.

Peggy found a parking space. She instructed Ann to tell go to Pam's room so they could put the clothes up they would be eventually be changing into. They didn't really know who room was closer. Peggy knew she just didn't want to be walking all outside on the parking lot and be detected on the cameras that watched over the patron's car and anything else they were watching. Peggy let Ann know that 5069 seemed a lot closer, so that's where they were headed to.

They knocked on the door. Pam immediately gave them the key to Dave's room. Peggy held the room key in her hand. She pointed to the bag as she said to Ann, "Ann. Look in my bag and get those two guns out, one for you and one Pam. Give me the blade, let's go."

Chapter 2

"This bitch is playing Smokey Robinson!" Peggy looked back at Kezia as they stood outside Dave's hotel room

"Baby come closer, ooh shit, and daddy this big dick is so good! All daddy, fuck this big pussy! That's right daddy, fuck that pussy!" The sound of Tara voice was louder than the music that was playing which was coming from the room

Peggy quietly slid the hotel key to unlock the door and slowly turned the handle on the door. She, Pam and Kezia made it in the room. Instead of the door closing quietly, Kezia had let the door slam. Dave slowly turned his head in the direction of the door. The way he was positioned the bed he couldn't move nothing but his lower body.

"What the fuck is going on? How the fuck did you get in here bitch?" Dave spoke aggressively. You could see smoke coming from his nostrils he was outraged with what was taking place at that moment.

"We're here for the fucking party. Nice going lil sis." Peggy went to hi-five Tara as she gathered herself and slowly coming up off of Dave's dick.

"What? You set me up bitch?" Dave tried to set up but wasn't able to move about the room as he pleased. He looked Tara dead in her face with vengeance, "And why is this whore calling you here sister?"

Tara stood put on her clothes and began to laugh, "Ah daddy I forgot to tell you that Peggy is my sister." She then turned to Kezia pointing to the bathroom, "Kezia, get his gun out of the bathroom."

"Damn Tara, the nigga let you handcuff him to the damn bed?" Peggy was very impressed with Tara tactics. She knew she had it in her but seeing it for herself was currently blowing her mind.

Tara walked over to kiss Dave on his forehead. Being that both of his hands were handcuffed she didn't have to worry about him trying to get up and attack her. She could see from the look in his eyes, that had he not been handcuff this situation would possibly be playing out very differently.

"Daddy, likes that freaky shit." Tara jerked back as Dave tried to raise up and take a bite out of her face. He went to kick her but she jumped back out of his reach.

"Dave, you know damn well not to fuck with my man." Peggy said as she stood close enough to him but not to close where he could probably kick the wind from her ass.

"Fuck you, bitch!" Dave said in a tone with fire following.

"Maybe in the next life, but not in this one, so Dave, all I can say to you right now is goodnight!" Peggy reached in for the kill. In seconds blood was gushing from his throat. His eyes were bucked and it was nothing else he could do. His mouth was wide open but there was not one sound that had escaped.

"Damn Peggy, what kind of blade is that? It almost cut his whole damn head off with one slice!" Kezia spoke and was caught off guard as she walked from out of the bathroom with Dave's gun in her hand.

"Get his ring and his watch." Tara said as she looked at his left arm. She didn't want to admit but all the blood had freaked her out.

Kezia start moving stuff around the room and she opened the drawer on the stand in which the TV was placed on. "Hey look at all this motherfucking money Pam, get that shit and let's go!"

"Wait Tara, you fucked that nigga?" Peggy said.

"So what?" Tara said wanting to get the fuck out of dodge.

"Here, Tara, grab this bag." Peggy handed her bag to Tara.

Tara looked inside the bag, "Why the fuck do you have a bottle of bleach in your bag? Who the fuck does that?" Tara frowned up from the thought.

"Bitch you just fucked this nigga and now he is dead! You are going to pour that bleach over him and all on that bed. You don't want your DNA left behind, do you?" Peggy spoke calmly.

Tara was glad that Peggy had thought that far ahead. She hadn't thought about DNA at all. She took her time as she made sure she pour that bleach on every inch of Dave and the bed.

Kezia was stun at the moment. Seeing an enormous amount of money had her frozen in her steps. The money made her forget all about the dead body that was currently in the room with them. She began thinking about all the things should go do. She looked at the neatly placed money and began to put it all the bag that was by the chair that was near the window in the hotel room. Pam walked over to help Kezia put the money in the bag. Pam was trying to count the stacks as they were placed in the bag.

"How much is that?" Peggy asked out of curiosity.

"Shit, this boy had over $350,000 in this drawer." Pam said.

"Bullshit! We got over $350,000 in that bag." Tara said as she put the empty bleach bottle back in the bag that Peggy had given to her.

"I like the way you talking!" Pam nodded her head in agreement with Tara.

Peggy looked out the door. She was checking to make sure no one was outside that could identify them leaving from the room. They headed back to the room where Ann was awaiting their arrival.

Ann had been looking out the window of the hotel room every second. She had the door unlocked where the latched held the door open. She wanted to make sure that the right individuals entered and not the wrong ones. However, she had something by her side if the wrong individual walked through the door.

Ann took the money out the bag and began to split if five ways. Everyone else was getting ready. They all began taking showers one after each other. They had something else on their agenda that needed their attention. The entire time Ann separated money and the girls were getting ready the room was quite. No one wanted to discuss the action that had just taken place.

Tara was the quietest one of all until it came to that ring and that watch. She sat their gazing at the items wondering who could she sale them to.

Peggy noticed how intrigued Tara was with the items in her hand, "I don't know what you are thinking. I know you rode some dick and you probably feel like that ring and watch is rightfully yours. I just want you to think about this. Everybody has seen Dave wearing that shit. The housekeeper is going to find Dave's body in the next few hours. That shit is going to be all over the news and people are going to be talking in the hood. The last thing you want out there in those streets is Tara trying to sale Dave's shit! We have a bag full of money. The best thing we can do is get rid of the shit. Let one of those base heads find that shit on Era."

Ann chimed in backing up Peggy. She knew that Peggy had a very good point. "Tara, if somebody see that shit, all hell will break lose. We got a shit load of money. Shit you can call that pain and suffering. Hell, wash yo pussy with that shit. Fuck that ring and that watch. You don't want nobody coming for your head for that bullshit!"

Tara looked over at the money and knew what they were telling her was correct. She grabbed a towel and began to wipe her finger prints of the jewelry.

"Let's get the fuck out of here because when they find his body, they are probably going to check everybody's room in the hotel." Peggy said.

Before the departure they knew that next meet up place would be the nightclub in the Midtown of St. Louis. The Loft was a mid-size club on Olive. Right outside the club you can find tricked out Escalades any night of the week. The who's who of the Lou would be shoulder to shoulder in the packed night club. All patrons can be found looking fly and fresh off a shoot for BET. The music and the sights would definitely be banging.

The girls didn't discuss what or who was next on the agenda. Peggy felt like she really didn't have to. It was no need for a plan. She knew once she took the lead, each one of them would step up and play their part. Then she quickly thought about it. She knew she might need to repeat somethings to Ann. Although, she knew Ann knew something happened to Dave, she just didn't know the details. Peggy and Ann had been friends for quite some time. Her trust solely belong with her sisters. They were the few people she didn't have to really worry about. She just wasn't so sure with Ann. But she knew just like Ann, if push came to a shove Ann life would most likely come to an end. As they exited the hotel room Peggy held Ann back.

"Ann when we get to the club, you don't know Tara. You don't even have to acknowledge me." Peggy informed Ann, then she turned to Tara, "Tara, while I take care of Tracey, you start kicking it with April. Pam and Kezia, already know to come back to their hotel room when we leave the club. Everybody else just go to our own homes. We'll meet up as my house by noon. Let's go Ann and don't leave those guns here."

Peggy thought it would be better if Ann just rode with her. When they got to the club they would just separate. Peggy wanted to make sure that Ann was comfortable with what was going on. She was basically keeping the enemy close, just in case.

"Peggy, you see that police, don't speed." Ann calmly said as she looked at the speedometer when she saw the police.

"I see those bitches." Peggy said in an I don't give fuck tone.

"Well slow the fuck down! We got all this money and these guns on us. Shit, don't forget we got this towel with this nigga jewelry in it." Ann thought about getting stopped by some local cops, who probably have pulled Dave over a thousand times. The twelve was represented with a D, the three was represented with an A, the six was represented with a V, and the nine was represented with an E. All the letter were diamonds. He had that watch customized to match the ring with Dave in diamonds sat in a black onyx plate on the gold ring. His watch and matching ring let all those who knew him or wanted to know him that his name was Dave.

"Every motherfucka in the Lou has either seen or heard about this jewelry." Ann said. She was thinking about how people even lied and said Jacob the Jeweler from New York had made this jewelry. Ann had to let out a chuckle from the stories that came with it and right now she would never know the truth about who or where it was made.

"Stop, laughing girl. What time is it?" Peggy said. She didn't care to ask why Ann was laughing.

"9:15, why you ask?" Ann looked over at Peggy.

"We got plenty of time throw this jewelry out." Peggy informed Ann.

"We're at?" Ann asked.

"We can throw it in one of those alleys that got a lot of trash in it? I am going to do down Era. We can get rid of it in the alley. It always look neglected as fuck in that alley. The motha-fucker always got trash everywhere." Peggy said as she began to turn down the alley. She turned the lights of to the truck so no one would be trying to figure out why she was going down the alley. She wasn't really worried because the people in the neighborhood would most likely think she was creeping looking and checking for Red.

Ann peeped a very good spot. They wanted someone to find it but they didn't want an easy find. They took the towel with the jewelry inside and sat it on fire. In seconds the whole entire trash can was on fire.

"Shit, the whole can is on fire!" Ann spoke with excitement.

"Good, let's go. Shit, let's go drop off the money at your house." Peggy said to Ann.

Ann was back in the truck. As Peggy pulled off they both were looking in the rearview mirror.

"Damn girl, look at all that smoke!" Ann said in amazement.

"I see it." Peggy said as she eased out the alley, looking up in the rearview mirror every few seconds. She was back on preparing her friend for the night, "Ann, after we been in the club about thirty minutes, you tell Tracey that you need to fix your make-up. Make sure that the bathroom is empty. When everything is clear, call my phone. Just say come in, if not say fuck it. Ann you go in first and I will be right behind you alright."

Peggy and Ann had made it on Olive. Peggy found the perfect parking spot. She was not that far from the door of the Loft. She told Ann to go in the club first. She watched Ann as she walked up to the Loft's door. Five minutes later Peggy went in the club.

Peggy seen Baby D. She could see why Ann was so attracted to him. His caramel skin tone complimented his gray eyes. His braids were neatly placed in rows on his head. He looked more like Michael Ealy when he was in Ice Cube's movie Barbershop.

Peggy looked all over the club, for Ann, from where she was standing. She even had to move around to make sure she had scanned the entire room. She held her cellphone in hand and kept checking to make sure she didn't miss her call.

Peggy was growing impatient, "Where the fuck is Ann? This club is packed!" As she surveyed the room she was trying to ignore and act like she didn't see Baby D approaching her.

"All shit! Hey, what's up Baby D?" Peggy said with a fake smile.

"Peggy, this is April and her friend Tara." Baby D introduced the girls that accompanied him.

"What's up April and Tara? Baby D, take care." Peggy was not for the small talk. She did not want to be seen around April. She walked away doing exactly what she was doing when Baby D approached her.

"Where the fuck is Ann?" Peggy looked over the club one more time. She was growing impatient. She looked back to make sure that April and Tara was in her sight but she was out of theirs. That's when she spotted Ann. "All, there she is." Peggy started walking over in Ann's direction. She walked in Ann's direction so that she could give her eye contact to let her know it was time to get started so they could leave.

When Ann saw Peggy, she made her way to the restroom. Peggy stood in the shadows and watched Ann. She watched as several women poured out the restroom. She wondered what Ann had said to get the women out the restroom so fast. Right as she was getting ready to pull out her phone to check it, it rang. Peggy put the phone up to ear. The person on the other end said exactly what she was waiting to hear.

"Come in." Ann whispered in the phone and waited for Peggy to hang up.

Right as Peggy was headed to the restroom. She was stopped in her tracks. The DJ was playing her song.

"That nigga would be playing my song right about now!" Peggy laughed to herself, still heading to the restroom.

She was disappointed that she couldn't go dance but she was cool at the same time. She smiled as she noticed that nearly the entire club was headed to the dance floor ready to get their shuffle on.

Peggy made it to the door right as Tracey was about to walkout. She thought to herself that this was going to be easier than she thought it would be.

"Hello, Tracey, going somewhere?" Peggy stopped her dead in her tracks.

"Why bitch?" Tracey said as spit followed the syllables as they rolled off her tongue.

"This whore!" was the sound right before the muffled sound that came from the silencer of that had been placed on the gun. Peggy tried to maintain her balance. The kick back and the power of the Magnum 44 made her stumble. She left off three more shots. Tracey died instantly. When Tracey seen Peggy's face she knew it was going to be trouble. She knew that Peggy held Red down and had his back no matter how much he played the field. Peggy looked in the mirror and noticed small blotches of blood on her face. She handed the gun to Pam as she blocked the door. She walked over to the paper towel holder and then to the sink. She wet the paper towel and began to wipe the blood from her face. Everyone stood in silence. Peggy pulled the gloves from her pocket and placed them on her hand. She then bent down and grabbed Tracey's body and pulled her in the last stall in the restroom.

Peggy looked Ann and Pam over. They both appeared shocked. Since it appeared that Peggy was the only one that maintained her cool, she looked Pam and Ann up and down to make sure there was no blood splatter or brain matter on them. They walked to the door, where Kezia was standing as a look out making sure no one came in. Peggy told Kezia they were going to head to the front door and she would call her phone when we made it. Peggy reiterated to her not to let anyone in there until they made it out the front door.

Peggy said to Kezia as she was about to walk toward the front of the club, "Tell them some two dudes are in there with some chick and they said give them five minutes."

As they were walking to the door, Baby D grabbed Pam by the wrist.

"Damn baby what's your name?" Baby D asked.

With one word she replied, "Pam."

"How you doing, Pam?" Baby D asked.

"Fine." Pam said.

"Are you here with your man?" Baby D kind of slurred his words.

Peggy had made it out the door. She was not about to stick around. Before she left she told Pam that he was part of the plan. So she stopped and talked. In seconds people were running towards the front door.

"Why are they running and screaming?" Baby D asked a random chick that was headed towards the door. "Hey baby what's going on?"

The women frantically answered, "It's a dead body in the bathroom!"

"What?" Baby D looked quite confused, but that didn't stop him from trying to get on the beauty that stood before him, "Let's get the fuck away from here! Pam, baby take my number down."

They exchanged numbers. Through the bustle and commotion Baby D yelled out to Pam, "Call me sexy."

Baby D let most of the people that were panicking pass him. When he noticed that the crowd was thinning out, he looked over at his partner and said, "Joe, let's ride!"

Kezia was very calm. She knew the killer had left the building but she wanted to mix in with the rest of the folks that were panicking. She grabbed Pam by her arm to get her attention.

"Pam, let's get the hell outta here." Kezia said as she walked and pulled Pam by the arm.

"I'm right behind you." Pam said as she and Pam were walking towards the door of the club. Once outside they both tried to remember where they had parked.

"Pam, here is the car." Kezia said as she pointed to Pam's rental car.

"Shit, everybody is trying to pull off at the same time. We are going to be all night trying to leave off this street." Pam said.

"Shit, look at all those police. The light red. I see it. There's Baby D and Joe." Kezia said as she pointed to the police, Baby D and Joe.

Baby D hadn't took his eyes off Pam. He had watched her out of the door. He kept his eyes on her as she and Kezia walked to the car. He rolled up right on the side of them.

Baby D got Pam's attention. He had let down his window and was waiting on her to let her window down. She barely had the window all the way down when he started talking.

"So, we meet again." Baby D said to Pam.

"I guess so." Pam returned with a smile.

"Would you and your peoples like to go out to eat?" Baby D asked.

"That's cool." Pam agreed.

Joe intervened, "What's your name?" he gave Kezia direct eye contact so that she knew he was talking to her.

"Kezia." Was all she said and she leaned back like she didn't want to be bothered. She was really trying to take in all the things that has occurred since she had touched down in St. Louis.

"Kezia! That sounds so damn sexy, but I like that though." Joe said.

Kezia looked over at him and smiled.

Baby D thought he could chime in and help his boy out, "Check this out, my man Joe like you." He waited on Kezia to respond.

Pam looked over at Kezia. She looked like she was in a whole other world. Pam slightly elbowed Kezia. Kezia jumped as though something had startled her. Kezia leaned up to get a perfect view of Joe. She chose her words carefully.

"Joe, you don't even know me to like me. But, I'm going to give you a chance to get to me know and see if you will be saying the same thing." Kezia winked her eye.

"Hey, follow us to Uncle Bills, the food is the best." Baby D said right before he pulled off to get in front of Pam and Kezia.

"Kezia, you see Joe checking you out?" Pam glanced over to Kezia as she barely took her eyes off the road. "That nigga is fine as hell. He straight goes pass go and collect two hundred dollars type fine. That nigga pass fine. He the prettiest nigga I've seen in years! I'm about to have all fun getting to know this mother-fucka."

"Pam, you crazy girl! Shit, Baby D cute too." Kezia felt the need to add that in there.

They had talked so much about how fine Baby D and Joe were that they hadn't even paid attention to the drive or the direction they had been lead to. The whole time they depended on Baby D to lead them to their destination. They had no clue of what part of town they were in, nor how they got there. They pulled on the parking lot of Uncle Bill's. The parking lot was small and tight.

They were approximately three cars away from Baby D and Joe. Pam noticed that they were waiting at the door.

"Come on girl, their waiting on us." Pam said to Kezia as she seen the boys standing by the door looking in their direction.

Uncle Bill's is a diner located on the south side of St. Louis. When you walk into the restaurant there were two sides. One side was for those just entering and waited to be seated. The other side was for those that were finish with their meal to pay and exit the facility. They were a twenty-four hour place of business. Uncle Bill's busiest hours were the a.m. hours. The clubs were closed and the hungry party people had a place to eat and continue to mingle. Having the best pancakes in the city was just a bonus. Breakfast, lunch and dinner meals are offered but they are best known for those pancakes.

The waitress with black and burgundy uniform walked over to seat them. She was very perky and her blonde ponytail bounced as she walked over the table to seat them. As they sat she placed four glasses of water from the tray she was holding in her hand. She asked them were they ready to order or did they need more time. Baby D let the waitress know that Pam and Kezia were first timers. She told them she would let them look over the menu and she would return.

Baby D wiggled in his seat and leaned closer to Pam, "Well, Pam, tell me something about you."

Pam smiled. She wondered if she should make up something or tell the truth, "Well, my name is Pamela Jones. I am from New York. I don't have any children. I don't drink or do rugs. I'm in nursing school."

Baby D laughed, "Damn Baby, you're a keeper!"

Joe looked over at Kezia. He wanted to know her resume, "Well Kezia, what about you?"

"I don't have kids and I'm a registered nurse." Kezia smiled.

The waitress approached, "Are you guys and gals ready to place your order?" The ponytail bounced right along with her perky personality.

"Pam, what would you like?" Baby D asked as they both looked over the menu.

Pam looked over at Baby D and gave him direct eye contact, "Why don't you order for me?"

Baby D looked at the waitress. He told her that they both would take steak, eggs and pancakes. He let her know he wanted American cheese on his eggs and he wanted his steak medium-well. Pam looked over at the waitress and let her know she would like the same.

The waitress turned to Kezia, "What about you Miss?"

Kezia nodded in Joe's direction, "He will order for me, too."

Joe just smiled as he placed his order, "We will have T-bone steaks. Both well done with eggs with cheese and the pancakes. We will also take two glasses of orange juice."

Both of the gentlemen, along with the ladies, thanked the waitress as she let them know she would put their order in quickly.

Joe wiggled in his seat, folded his arms and leaned back in the booth, "So, how long have you two been here in St. Louis?"

Kezia looked at Pam. The eye contact they made with each other let Pam know that Kezia would take it from here.

Kezia looked at both the guys, "We got here today."

Joe didn't even let her finish, "Well, how do you all like it so far?"

Kezia looked directly into Joe's eyes, "Well since I met you, I love it here! I think I may never go back home."

Kezia looked around, "Someone's phone ringing!"

Baby D looked down at his side and grabbed his phone, "Yeah, what's up April?"

Baby D was quiet and wrinkles formed on his forehead. His lips were tight and he placed his hand on his forehead. Joe was all ears.

"You bullshitting me, that's fucked up, I'll holla at you later on." a tear rolled from the corner of his right eye. "Joe, man that was Tracey that they found dead at the Loft." Baby D put his head down and covered his face with both of his hands.

Joe, asked, "Tracey, who?" He only knew one Tracey but he didn't want it to be that Tracey. He only needed confirmation.

Baby D replied with pain in his voice, "Dave's old lady. You know they just found Dave dead in a hotel room. Shit wicked out here! Folks ain't seen or heard shit! It's like a motherfucking ghost has come into town just murking shit."

"Damn! Why his gal get killed? We was right in that joint, too!" Joe looked at Baby D for some clarification. He tried to read his face and all he could see was pain.

"She said she was shot in the head. April said Pete is fucked up. He talking about leaving town." Baby D just shook his head in disbelief.

Joe interjected, "Man that sounds like a drug deal gone bad. Baby D, that's why I tell you to be careful how you talk to people. Here comes our food now."

Pam and Kezia couldn't even look in each other's direction. They kept their eyes on the gentlemen that were discussing the crime they were very familiar with.

"Where are you staying?" Joe didn't want to show how fucked up behind the murder he was. Baby D on the other hand was quiet. He barely touched his food.

"At the hotel not far from the airport." Pam didn't want to say the hotel. She had seen several hotels in that area, she just couldn't remember the names. She just knew the hotel where Dave was killed and she knew she was definitely not about to say that hotel.

"Kezia, can I call you sometimes?" Joe asked.

"You sure can." Kezia said trying to maintain her composure.

"What's your number?" Joe asked.

Kezia answered quickly with the correct number, "226-1944."

"Baby, is that area code 718, 212, 347, or 314?" Joe had to let her know he knew something about the state she claimed she was from.

Kezia looked at him and smile, "It's a 314 number. I got this phone today because I lost my phone at the airport. I sat it down when I went to TSA checkpoint."

"What about you Pam, can I have your number?" Baby D looked up at Pam with the deepest hurt in his eyes.

Pam sort of felt his pain. She was partially responsible but she knew she had a plan that she had to follow. She looked him in his eyes and with sincerity in her voice she said, "Sure sweetheart."

"Wait a minute!" Baby D grabbed his phone from his hip, "Let me put it in my phone."

Joe grabbed the tab and stood up, "Well ladies we both hate to end this lovely evening that we are having, but we have business to take care of." He turned to Kezia and said, "Kezia can I have a kiss, baby?"

Kezia stood to respond, "Anytime."

She kissed him liked she had known him.

Joe felt a tingle from that kiss, "Damn baby! That kiss tasted better than candy."

Pam thought about how they didn't know where they were. She looked over at Baby D and he was looking like he had lost his best friend. She didn't really want to bother him. She looked over to Joe as we was about to walk towards the front door, "Joe, can you tell us how to get to the highway?"

Joe thought about them not being from St. Louis and they had literally just followed them from a club. He wanted to say something about how did they find their way to the Loft. He quickly changed his mind and said, "Just follow behind us alright."

Joe paid the bill. He and Baby D got into their car and waited on Pam and Kezia to get in theirs. He led them straight to the highway. Kezia and Pam was quiet the entire ride. The only sound was the tires rolling on the pavement.

When Kezia saw the hotel from the highway she spoke, "Girl, hurry up and get to the hotel so I can take damn cold shower."

"Damn, that kiss fucked you up like that?" Pam laughed at Kezia.

Kezia quickly shot back, "Fuck you bitch!"

They shared a laugh as Pam pulled onto the parking lot of their hotel. Pam went to her room and got straight into the shower. She then called Kezia's room. "Hey girl, you in the bed? I've just gotten out of the shower."

"Me, too." Kezia said.

"I am on my way to your room. Open the door alright." Pam said to Kezia.

Pam made it to Kezia's room in under a minute flat. Kezia had the door open and was waiting on her to enter.

Pam looked Kezia in her face. She tried to read her but she was having a very hard time. Pam took a deep breath, "Girl, I don't feel right being at this hotel. We are going to have to move somewhere else because I can't sleep here. I can't get Baby D's face expression out of my head. This would be too ironic. The same day we get here his homeboy's dies and we at the same damn hotel." Pam shook her head, "we gotta go."

The phone began to ring. Pam looked at Kezia. She knew it wasn't her phone because she left her phone in her room.

Kezia walked over the stand and grabbed the phone as if she were scared of it, "That's my phone. Who is calling me at this time of night?" She took a brief pause and spoke, "Hello?"

"Hey baby were you sleep?"

"Naw, I just got out of the shower. What made you call me tonight?" Kezia asked out of curiosity.

"I was just thinking about you." Joe said.

"That's nice." Kezia smiled.

"When can I see you again?" Joe asked.

"Just tell me when and I'm there." Kezia didn't want to make plans and Peggy had other plans. She knew if he set the time and she informed every one of the plan, it shouldn't be a problem where she would have to miss the date.

"Sunday, we can go out to dinner and to the club." Joe informed her of the arrangements.

"Well," Peggy paused, "dinner is cool but after tonight, I don't think I'm going to anymore clubs here in St. Louis."

"All baby, don't be like that! You going to be with me. We are going ballroom dancing so dress after five." Joe let her know that was not the type of scene they would partake in this time around.

"That sounds nice. Who are we going with?" Kezia asked.

"Just you and me. I get to have you all to myself. Yeah Baby D, don't go places like that. Kezia, how is it living in New York?" Joe asked.

"It's cool but its fast living. Why do you ask?"

"I was just asking." Joe said nonchalantly.

"Joe, tell me something about you." Kezia said.

"Well, I was born in St. Louis. I have two sisters and three brothers. My mother raised us by herself, working two jobs. My daddy ran the streets all the fourteen years old was. My sister, Tina, quit school and got a job so we can all stay together. She kept all the bills paid but we didn't' have money for food. So, I started selling drugs to help around the house. I put my brother and sister through school and moved my sister Tina moved to California so she can be with my other sister and brothers. Everyone left St. Louis and is doing well. I think it's time for me to leave." Joe felt comfortable telling her his story.

"Why?" Kezia asked as she watched Pam as she was about to fall asleep in the chair on the side of the desk.

"Because all this killing, fuck that! I want to get married and have kids and enjoy life." Joe thought about a lavish peaceful lifestyle.

"Well Joe, when are you gonna give the up the drug life?" Kezia asked.

"Very soon." Joe said.

"Do you want kids?" Kezia really wanted to get to know him. He seem like a guy that was really worth getting to know. She knew it would be against the rules of the game but it was something that attracted her to him.

"Yes, I want to have several kids." Joe thought about his brothers and sisters.

"What about Baby D, you gonna leave him behind?" Kezia needed to know just how close he and Baby D were.

"Kezia, what I'm about to tell you stays just between us, alright." He didn't even wait for her to respond. He continued to talk, "Baby D and his girlfriend Ann are going through some crazy shit. That's going to send somebody to jail or somebody is going to get killed."

Kezia interrupted, "What do you mean his girlfriend, and he took Pam out to eat?"

Joe tried to clean it up so he could finish confiding in Kezia, "His ex-girlfriend, her name is Ann. She took some money from him. She thinks Baby D don't know she got it. So, he took her car back that he gave her and whipped her ass and made his cousin beat her ass."

Hearing Ann had money already intrigued Kezia, "Damn, how much money can a woman take from a man to make him beat her ass?"

Joe was having pillow talk without the pillow, "She took 200,000 thousand dollars from him. And I don't want to be in that bullshit because something bad is gonna happen. That's why I'm outta here in about three months. I got money and my life, it's time to go."

"Where are you going?" Kezia was naturally interested.

"I am not going to say where I'm going, but I would like to keep in touch with you."

"That's fine. Joe, it's six in the morning, we better get some sleep."

"Kezia, what we talked about is just between us."

"Okay Joe, nice talking to you."

"Pam, wake up! Girl, get up!" Kezia shook Pam as she slept in the chair.

"What?" Pam woke up.

"Something's not right!" Kezia said.

"What the fuck you talking about?" Pam asked.

" You know I was on the phone with Joe, he said Ann stole $200,000 thousand dollars from Baby D and the bitch April is his cousin."

"What?" Pam tried to make sense of what she was hearing.

"Yeah!" Kezia said.

"That's why they jumped on her and he took his car back." Pam said as she put two and two together, "Kezia, Joe told you that?"

"Yes!"

"We need to talk to Peggy, something is not right." Pam said.

"Well when we get to her house today, I'll tell her what Joe said." Kezia assured Pam.

"Fuck that, give me the phone." Pam didn't want to wait. She grabbed Kezia's phone and dialed Peggy's number, "Hello. Peggy, is Red there?"

"Why?" Peggy needed to know why was her man whereabouts was any concern.

Pam didn't even think about what she was asking. She just wanted to really know would Peggy be able to talk. She felt if Red was there that the conversation would have to wait. She was so anxious that she couldn't explain that, "Is he there?" fell from her lips in a very demanding tone.

Hearing the tone in her voice, Peggy had no alternative but to answer, "Yeah."

Pam was hoping he was not there. Finding out that he was changed what she was about to say, "We need to talk. Now!"

Peggy wanted to know but she was not about to talk in front of Red. "Pam, can it wait?"

Pam remained calm. "No! I also need you to call Tara, but don't call Ann."

Peggy was not sure what to think or what was Pam on but her curiosity grew stronger. Not trying to talk too much around Red she kept her questions brief, "Why not?"

Pam was anxious to feel Peggy in but she knew over the phone was not the time, "Just don't!" Pam said to Peggy.

Now Peggy was ready to find out what the hell was really going on right now, "Pam, call Tara on your phone." Peggy said to Pam.

Peggy told Pam she was about to call Tara. She let her know that she was about to tell Tara that they were going to meet them at the hotel. They both hung up the phone. Kezia asked Pam questions about what did Peggy say and how did she sound. Pam let her know that she wasn't really tripping off all that. She informed Kezia that Tara and Pam would be there in thirty minutes.

Peggy patted her foot on the floor as she listened to Tara's phone ring. She was growing highly impatiently as she listened to the sound of the phone ringing.

"Hello." Tara said.

"Bitch! You keep that phone in your motherfucking hand at all times. What the fuck took you so long to answer the damn phone?" Peggy said the force.

"Bitch! I was shitting. I don't take the phone to the bathroom with me. What the fuck do you want anyway?" Tara said slightly irritated. She had hurried to wipe herself just to get to the damn phone. She was trying to get back to the toilet. Barely holding the phone because she didn't wash her hands, she was ready to hang up.

"Pam, wants us to meet her and Kezia at their hotel room. It has to be important because Pam couldn't, well she wouldn't talk on the phone about it." Peggy informed Tara.

Tara let Peggy finished before she spoke, "Well girl you can come get me because I have to hop in the shower. How long will it take you get here?"

"Bitch, I am on my way now. I should be there in fifteen minutes. No later than 10!" Peggy said as she walked towards her front door.

"Bet!" Tara said as she press end and ran back to the bathroom.

Peggy made it to Tara's place in ten minutes flat. They made it to the hotel in twenty minutes. The car was barely put in park as they both hopped out the car headed to Pam and Kezia.

Peggy tapped on the door and Pam opened it before Peggy removed her hand from the door. Barely in the room, Peggy said, "Now, what is this all about?"

Kezia looked directly at Peggy, "Joe, told me some shit and it's just not adding up."

Tara looked at Peggy then at Kezia, "What the fuck did he say?"

Kezia told them everything Joe told her. She had even began with how she was about to go to sleep and she wanted to know who would be calling her in the wee hours of the morning.

"Kezia, are you sure that's what he said?"

"Tara, I taped everything he said." Kezia rolled her eyes.

"Well Peggy, I found out the April and Baby D are cousins. I was waiting till we got to your house to tell you. And, the word on the street is Dave was getting ready to reload. That's why he was at the hotel with all that money. And Ann said, the nigga had $350,000 dollars. But on the streets they said he had $500,000 dollars on him." Kezia said.

"Did Ann count the money by herself?" Peggy asked.

"Yeah." Pam chimed in.

"We are going to hold out on killing Baby D for a while. I am gonna set his bitch up and see what happen. The bitch better not be playing the cross game! Pam and Kezia, whenever I say something bad about Baby D and Joe, both of you bite my head off. Tara, keep your eyes on Ann at all times. Just in case that bitch is playing the snake game, I'm gonna stay ten steps ahead of her ass. Where's my phone?" Peggy began to look around.1

"Right here." Tara handed her phone to her.

Peggy looked at her battery percentage, "Shit! My phone needs to be fixed, it keeps losing juice."

"Here, you can use my phone." Tara said as she was about to give Peggy her phone to use.

"I'm cool. You can just dial this number for me and see if they answer." Peggy said.

Pam and Kezia just looked at Peggy and Tara. They both were trying to figure out what was going on and what would be their next move. Peggy wasn't saying much but her face showed that she was thinking very hard about what she had just heard. Tara was a hard read for them. Tara looked as though she was untroubled and didn't have a care in the world.

"Dial 901-945-3878." Peggy told Tara.

Tara stood from the bed and handed Peggy her cell phone, "Here Peggy it's ringing."

Peggy grabbed the phone and placed it up to her ear, "Hello, are you sleeping?"

"Yeah who is this?" The person that Peggy called shot back.

"Peggy." She said as though the person on the other end of the phone should have automatically known it was her.

"Hey, sis what's up?" the chic on the other end of Tara's phone said.

"I need you to come up here." Peggy said.

"For what now, Peggy?" Peggy sister Sherry wanted to know what type of shit her sister was about to get her involved in or with. She was down because Peggy always looked out for her. She really wanted to know did she have come like now or a day or two later.

"I'll tell you when you get here and bring Paul with you. But don't tell anybody that you are coming up here. I need you and Paul up her by Monday." Peggy told her sister.

"Shit Peggy it's Sunday? What you need us up there for?" Sherry just needed to know who or what was the problem. She knew it had to be a problem because that's when Peggy called. She never called to say hi or see how someone was doing. She only called when she needed something.

"Don't you want to kick it with your sister?" Peggy tried to make as though she didn't want nothing. It would just be something when she got to the Lou.

"That's some bullshit! But I'll be up there." Sherry already knew Peggy was running game. Her love for her sister made her agree to come.

"Where's Paul?" Peggy asked about her brother.

"In the room sleep." Sherry looked at Paul lay in his bed. She could see him as she sat on the couch.

"Give him the phone." Peggy said.

Sherry got up from her comfortable seat. She knew if she wanted Paul money would be involved. Peggy already knew that Paul wasn't moving if the price wasn't right. Sherry knew it as well. Peggy didn't have to attach price. That was understood when she said Paul's name. Sherry touched Paul. He was a light sleeper. He opened his eyes and Sherry handed him the phone.

"Who dis?" Paul said as he placed the phone up to his ear.

"What's up big brother?" Peggy asked Paul.

"You tell me?" Paul said with a groggy voce.

"I need you to come up here with Sherry in the morning." Peggy said in a seductive desperate voice.

"You know I'm down. I just need to know what the deal is." Paul continued thinking about a previous incident, "You know I'm not with that dumb shit."

"It's this girl I want you to get on. And I don't want her to know that you're my brother." Peggy said.

"She got some money because this dick cost money." Paul said as he grabbed his manhood.

Sherry had been standing there the entire time. She wanted to hear what was going on. When Paul grabbed himself. Sherry rolled her eyes and left Paul to finish the phone call alone.

"She has a few dollars." Peggy chuckled.

"She got kids." Paul wanted to know if he was gonna have to play the role of I'm the best stepdad you want for your kids.

"No." Peggy keep it brief.

"Well, I need new clothes and shoes." Paul was about to ice this entire situation for what it was worth.

"Don't worry, we got you." Peggy said.

"Who the fuck is we?" Paul asked.

"Me, Tara, Pam and Kezia." Peggy looked around the room at each person as she said their name.

Paul rose up from his resting position, "All shit, what the fuck is going on?"

Peggy laughed, "I just want to trick this girl out of some info and $240,000 dollars."

"Shit, if she go that kind of money, I'll be there tonight!" Paul got and walked to meet Sherry in the kitchen.

"Bye Paul, I'll see you later." Peggy laughed.

"Hey, have Tara and Kezia there when we get there." Paul said.

"They'll be here." Peggy informed him.

"Alright sis, later." Paul hung up the phone.

"Let's go, don't anybody say a word to Ann about shit. Because it might be a setup on Baby D's end." Peggy said.

"Peggy, don't you know where they get their shit from?" Tara asked.

Peggy began to speak proudly, "Yeah, Wayne ass."

"Well, you know Wayne likes you?" Tara said as though that was a plus to help their situation out.

"No, Wayne wants to fuck me! But, I'm going to fuck with his head. Red is going out of town today and while he's gone, I'm gonna fuck with Wayne's mind. Tara, at 11:00, you call Ann and tell her we are going to me at 5:00 at my house."

Kezia and Pam wanted to know where this Wayne conversation was going. They both just kept quiet because they both knew eventually either Peggy or Tara would disclose some more information. They just sat and followed the conversation.

"Shit, what if Wayne doesn't take the bait?" Tara asked.

"I'll kick his punk ass! But the nigga gonna talk." Peggy looked down once her cell phone began to ring, "All shit, this Red calling."

Peggy hadn't even said hello. Red spoke once he heard that the phone had stopped ringing, "Yeah baby where you?"

Peggy began her lie, "We just left the boat. I'll be there in 20 minutes."

"I'm on my way to the airport now." said Red.

"I'm sorry baby. I wanted to fuck the shit out of your before you left. I love you." Peggy put her head down so the girls wouldn't be looking down her throat.

"I love you more." Red said and brought the phone call to an end.

Peggy hopped up. She needed to contact Wayne. She looked at the girls, "Alright everybody, be at my house at 3:00 sharp. When you call Ann and ask where am I, tell her that I'm with Red. Tara, you go with me and watch my back alright."

Kezia stood up, "Fuck this shit. We are all in this shit together."

Peggy looked at Kezia, "Alright, keep a low profile. Tara, if I'm not out of there in one hour, come in that motherfucker shooting everything walking."

Peggy just figured she would just show up at Wayne's front door. She drove alone. Tara, Pam and Kezia were in the same car. They slowly followed behind her. Tara noticed she was headed towards North County. Tara had been to Wayne's house a couple of times with Peggy but she couldn't remember where his house was located. Apparently, Peggy couldn't either. She had pulled over. They noticed that she had pulled her phone out.

Tara looked down and noticed that Peggy was calling her. She picked up her phone, "Hello."

"Tara, do you remember where the fuck does Wayne live on Chambers?" Peggy said.

Tara couldn't believe she had asked her that question. She wasn't the one fucking with him. Why would where he stay be important to her was all she could think but she wouldn't dare say that to Peggy.

Peggy noticed that Tara hadn't answered her question, "Let me call you back and call this nigga."

Tara ended the call before Peggy pressed end. Speaking in the atmosphere, Tara said, "That's what the fuck you should have done at first instead of calling my fucking phone."

"Hello." Wayne said. He was excited to see Peggy name scroll across the screen. That was one phone call he had been waiting on for quite some time.

"Hey handsome." Peggy wanted to pour it on thick but she decided against it.

"Who is this sounding all sexy as hell?" Wayne was just playing a game. He had her name locked in.

"This Peggy."

"Hey, baby what's happening?" Wayne said.

"I'm on Chambers and I thought about you. I started to just pop up and knock on your door, but I can't remember the house." Peggy was so serious. She was kind of upset with herself.

"Girl, how could you forget that? I'm at 14037 Chambers."

"Cool. I'll be there in 10 minutes, be outside." Peggy told Wayne and ended her call.

Peggy called Tara back. Tara sat and looked at Peggy's name for a few seconds before she answered. She was glad she had placed her phone on vibrate. Pam and Kezia wouldn't be looking at her like answer the fucking phone bitch!

"Yeah." Tara spoke with an attitude.

"Y'all follow me. I want you all to park a few cars down from the house. Give me about twenty minutes and then call and check on me. If I don't answer, you all come in that motherfucking house and smoke everything that moves!" Peggy was so serious and Tara knew it.

Wayne was standing outside like Peggy had said. Pam rode pass and circled the block. She didn't want to just pull up and park while Wayne was standing there.

"Well how have you been doing?" Wayne asked.

"Fine baby?" Peggy responded.

"So, you didn't forget today's my birthday?" Wayne smiled.

"Boy please, I just been thinking about you, I didn't know today was your birthday." Peggy blushed.

"It's not. I was just fucking with you." Wayne said as he led Peggy through the front door of his home.

"Have a seat." Peggy sat down as instructed.

"Were you on your way out?" Peggy asked.

"I was just watching the news. Did you know they found Dave dead at a hotel by the airport?" Wayne studied her face.

"Dave who?" Peggy was emotionless as she asked him the question.

"Dave that drove that black BMW." Wayne said.

"I think I know him." Peggy head a dumb look and seemed to be very unsure of who he was speaking about.

"Then somebody killed his girlfriend Tracey. Did you know his girl?" Wayne asked.

Peggy avoided the question, "Damn, that was fucked up! It's too many snakes out here. Shit, Saint Louis, that's snake city. And the girls are snaking worse than the niggas."

"Like that bitch Ann that Baby D is fucking wit, that's one dumb whore. She stole $200,000 from him. Talking about some friend of hers that live in Ladue is keeping it for her. Talking about it was in her car and the police got behind her so she went to her friend's house and left it there. Now she is talking about the bitch is playing games with the money. The bitch is going to show Baby D where the house is today."

Peggy tried to keep her composure. She wanted to tell Wayne that she was the bitch that stayed in Ladue. She was glad that Red told her that everyone didn't need to know where they stayed. At that moment she hated that Ann knew. She didn't know how Ann showing Baby D where she stayed would pan out.

"Wayne, that sounds like some bullshit to me!" Peggy said to Wayne.

"It sounds like bullshit to me, too. But, it's not about the money cause he can make that back." Wayne looked over at Peggy's phone. It had rang for the fifth time. He couldn't ignore it any longer, "Why your phone keeps ringing?"

Peggy looked at Wayne. "This my sister she's just checking up on me." Peggy pressed answer, "I'm good. I will hit you up when I get to my car."

Wayne waited for the call to end before he spoke, "Well you know Peggy you should have been my wife. I have been in love with you since we were kids. But I'm glad that we are still good friends."

Peggy smiled, "Wayne, we will always be friends, you're like a brother to me."

"Peggy, you know you are the only one I can talk to and keep it real with."

"I'm glad you feel that way. I better leave before my man come looking for me. But, Wayne, just say fuck the money before somebody gets killed."

"Peggy, I can't see letting her get over like that! She is going to get what's coming to her. I'll think about it," said Wayne. "But thanks Peggy."

"For what?" Peggy didn't understand what he was thanking her for.

"For just listening to me." Wayne said with a sincere look in his eyes.

"Anytime. Bye Wayne, give me a hug. Later lil brother." Peggy reached to give him a hug.

"That's big brother, don't play!" Wayne said as he embraced her.

"So this bitch wants to play the cross game?" Peggy said to herself as she walked back to her car. She looked to see if the girls were still there and they were.

Peggy drove like crazy trying to get to her home in Ladue. Pam was trying her best to keep up. No one said nothing but they were all trying to figure out why was Peggy driving as though she was a Nascar driver.

"Damn, I wish these people would drive." Peggy said as she swerved through traffic. She was at her home in a split second. Pam had did her best to keep up. When Peggy made it to her front door, Pam was pulling up in her driveway. Peggy left the door open so they could walk right in the house. Before anyone could ask a question Peggy was giving out instructions.

"Tara, call Sherry and Paul." Peggy demanded.

"What's wrong?" Tara asked. Tara was trying to figure out why the hell Peggy wasn't making this phone call herself.

Peggy looked at them as they were looking at her, "We'll talk after I get off the phone."

"Hello." Sherry said.

"When will you be here?" Peggy asked.

"In a few minutes. Peggy, we are about twenty-five minutes away from you." Shelly said as she sat on the passenger side while Paul did all the driving.

"Cool. That's even better. I'll see you when you get here." Peggy began to pace back and forth.

"Pam, call Ann and tell her Red got family biz ok. Everybody, pull the cars around to the back and let me think." Peggy head began to hurt. Her thoughts were moving a mile a minute.

"Peggy, what's going on?" Tara asked.

"Kezia and Pam check out of the hotel, I'm moving you to Red's family house. Paul and Sherry will be here in about fifteen minutes so go check out and don't leave anything behind and come right back here! Go now and change cars, don't get trucks, get cars." Peggy informed them. She had to remove everything she could remember that Ann was aware of them doing, living and driving.

"Damn Tara, roll me a blunt." Peggy said.

"Peggy, what the fuck is wrong with you?" Tara needed to know. She just couldn't sit in limbo.

"That bitch told Baby D that his money is over her friend's house out in Ladue and her friend is playing games every time she calls about the money." Peggy pulled smoke from her neatly rolled blunt.

"Oh fuck this! I'm blowing this bitch head off!" Tara was pissed.

"Nah, I got a plan for her. Here comes Paul and Sherry." Peggy could hear them talking as they approached the door.

"You sure that's them?" Tara was slightly paranoid.

"I know my sister and brother, let them in." Peggy pointed to the door.

"Hey sis, how are you doing?" Sherry said to her sister.

"Fine." Peggy said to her sister and turned towards her brother, "Nigga if you walk pass me and not give me a hug, and I'll shoot yo ass!"

"Pam and Kezia are back already." Tara said as she stood in the window looking outside.

As they walked through the door, Peggy got in big sister mode, "Did you all get everything?" She waited on them to confirm they had retrieved all their belongings from the hotel.

Peggy thought about what Wayne had said. It was time to let Kezia know that Joe was telling the truth, "Joe told you the truth, Kezia!"

"You bullshitting me?" Kezia knew he had no reason to lie to her about something she really didn't know about.

"The whore had him thinking I had the money. This bitch is getting ready to feel me! This bitch is going to think I'm the motherfucking mob. Sherry, you are going to stay here with me and

Red." Peggy was discombobulated. Her thoughts were all over the place.

"Who the fuck is Red?" Sherry asked.

"My husband, Sherry." Peggy said.

Tara laughed, "Black as his ass is they should call that nigga Blue!"

Everybody start to laugh.

Peggy had caught an attitude, "Well the blacker the berry, the sweeter the juice! Plus that nigga can fuck so damn good, he needs a fucking Grammy and he's rich! Now, get back to biz. Paul, Kezia is going to have to take you to get a car." Peggy went from a hundred to zero real quick.

"Paul, you are going to stay at my house on Spring Garden. I want you to find out everything about Ann and where is she keeping her money and what are her plans. I want to know everything that bitch does. When she eats, when she shits, everything! Tara you take Paul shopping and get him some shoes, clothes and make sure that nigga smells good every day. So get him some Unforgettable by Sean John. Snatch up some Kenneth Cole and some Prada for men and some Issey Miyake. Take my Visa, spend every dime on him."

"What's the limit?" Tara asked.

"Fifty grand. He needs to look and smell like money." Peggy said.

"Damn! What this bitch do?" Paul was excited about his little shopping spree he was about to partake in.

"Paul, you're going to act like you're a big trick. Tell her your wife left you, and ran off with the kids and half of your money. If she asks what kind of work you do, tell her that you are a chef. Today is Sunday and she always go the Best Steakhouse on Grand for dinner. She gets there about 6pm. Here's a picture of what she looks like. When you see her, you will know who she is. Paul, take this money so the bitch and think you have all money. Tara, you stick to April like white rice. Pam, get all the way on Baby D, suck that nigga dick, fuck him, even blow up his ass if you have, too. I need to know at all times what that man is thinking. Kezia and you do the same." Peggy let the instructions she was giving to her family just roll off her tongue. Her family was trying their best to keep up with all what she was saying.

Peggy looked at her sister, "Sherry, you stay around the house and answer the phone. When Ann calls, always tell her I'm not home. When she comes over here, never let her see you."

"Why not?" Sherry asked.

"Sherry, I'm paying you to do what I ask you to do. So, do that! Please lil sister?" Peggy pleaded.

"Paul, let Sherry see that flick so when she comes over here, she will know to stay away." Peggy pointed to make sure Paul gave her the picture.

Sherry took a look at the picture and her faced expression was not pleasing to her on lookers. Sherry began to speak very loudly, "This is not her!"

"Yes, it is!" Peggy spoke with major confidence.

"Bullshit! Her name is Robin!" Sherry shot back.

"What you mean her name is Robin?" Peggy retorted.

Sherry needed to let her sister know that she knew what she was talking about, "Peggy, I went to college with her in Ohio. Her man name is Tray Bag, the nigga lives in Texas. That's where she just bought a house about two weeks ago. That bitch has been setting niggas up for a while."

"Wait! Give us the rundown of her family Sherry." Paul needed to know what type of situation he was about to walk into.

Sherry continued, "Well, her name is Robin Pipes and her sister name is Monica. She has a brother name Eric. They all work together. Those motherfuckers go from city to city putting in work on dope boys!"

Peggy took in all what Sherry had said. She got what she felt was important out of that conversation. She looked over at Paul. She chose her words very carefully.

"Paul, I want this bitch to think you are her next victim. I know yo stunting ass can pull this off. I want you to floss so motherfucking hard on her ass! When you around this bitch make her think she can have whatever she likes!"

Paul had left and was on his mission. Just as his sister said, she came waltzing into the Best Steak House at six sharp. She spotted him as soon as she walked through the door. She was trying not to give him too much eye contact but it was hard. She peeped his Presidential Rolex and knew he had to be a Rapper or a dope boy. About three hours later Paul was back at Peggy's house.

"Peggy, I'm back." Paul spoke in a honey I'm home type of voice.

"Paul, did you see her?" Peggy was anxious to know did Ann take the bait.

"I saw her. She gave me her phone number. We chit chatted about nothing but she couldn't keep her eyes off my time piece."

"Cool. I'll move you in your new house in the morning. After you come back from getting you a new car, I'll will show you how to get to your new house and back here. When are you getting up with her?" Peggy waited on his response.

"I'm going to cook for her and then I'm going to fuck her the same night! And then two days later, I'll call and tell her I want to come and spend some time with her." Paul was ready to take it to the next level.

"And make sure you leave her door unlocked so I can get in. She has a safe, see if you can find it." Peggy thought about how she never seen the safe, but she knew it existed.

"Alright, sis." Paul was excited. He had done many slick and shiesty things for his sister. This right here took the cake.

"And make sure you cover up ole boy." Peggy wanted to make sure her brother practiced safe sex.

Time was going by so fast. Nothing had popped off. Baby D hadn't shown up in Ladue. Peggy didn't know what to think but her plan was not about to change.

"Paul, you have been seeing her for the past two months now."

"Baby girl been playing hard to get. But she's coming over here so I can follow her to her house so I can spend the weekend with her. Her safe is in the basement in the back and combination number is 37 left, 13 right, and 7 left. Peggy, the girl got big money in that safe! And a gun." Paul gave his sister what she wanted.

"I'll be there about 8:30. Make sure the door is unlocked." Peggy had to make sure her brother was on point with what was about to go down.

Peggy looked at Tara. "Girl, I can't wait until tonight. Paul has planned that he will be at her house tonight for the weekend. I can't wait to see her face. I can't wait to see what's in that safe and the look on her face when she sees me. And the look on her face when she finds out that Paul's our brother! She just looking at the fact that he's light-skinned and he has hazel brown eyes with good hair and that he's bow-legged. Not to mention that he has pretty white ass teeth. That's a plus. She's looking how fine his ass is. That simple minded bitch is trying to play the cross game, the whore forgot who gave her the game!" Peggy had rambled for so long, Tara forgot what they were initially talking about.

"What time are we leaving here?" Tara asked Peggy.

"At 8:00." Peggy said.

"Well let's get dressed because it's 7:47 now." Pam said.

"Oh shit! Let's get ready everybody. Wear jeans and tennis shoes. We going in two different cars and make sure we get Paul out first before we do anything. Let's go Tara, you ride with me."

They were out the house and on the road headed to Ann's house. Peggy looked up in her rearview mirror. "Pam and Kezia don't drive too close on me." Peggy said as if they could hear her.

"Shit the police is out here!" Tara said as she noticed seven police cars in less than five minutes.

"Call Pam and tell her to slow down." Peggy said as she continue to watch what was in front of her and what was behind her in her rearview.

"Pam, you think you in New York, slow down!" Tara laughed.

"Shut the fuck up! I'm dong 75 miles per hour." Pam retorted.

"Bitch! This St. Louis, the speed limit is 55." Tara said in as if you didn't know type of tone.

"All shit, okay, why are you going through the alley? Paul left the door unlocked. Pull down the alley some." Pam asked.

"Peggy, do I get to do this one?" Sherry asked.

"Sherry, what are you doing here?" Peggy asked.

"I want to see her face when Ann finds out that this girl she's been talking about is my sister." Sherry chuckled.

"You know that JJ having nineteen kids works out in a crazy way! Everybody ready, let's go! Turn your cell phones off." Peggy said as her crew headed to Ann's door.

"Oh yeah because Baby D calls too much!" Kezia laughed.

"No more than Joe does." Pam shot back.

"Ooh Paul that feels so good. Paul, go deeper." Ann was in the grove and not knowing at the time no one was listening to her but Paul.

"Oh baby, this some good pussy!" Paul was in the grove. She was wet just liked he liked it.

"Paul, this your pussy!" Ann was talking shit. But, how he had her feeling at the time, she meant every word.

"Wait, sit on this dick." Paul wanted Ann to ride him like she was at the rodeo.

"Oh shit, this hurt! Your dick is so motherfucking big!" Ann tried to ease down on it.

"Work that pussy on this dick! Show me how much you love this dick." Paul was enjoying every minute of sex with Ann.

Ann couldn't say the same. To her he was tearing up her insides, "Let me give you some foreplay, alright? Daddy, let me show you how this big dick is supposed to be sucked!"

"Girl, what you doing, aw shit, an Ann you the best! I'm getting ready to nut! OH girl this feels to damn good! Here it comes! Baby, take all of it!" Ann was swallowing his unborn seeds.

"Are you having fun, Ann?" Peggy asked as she watch Ann wipe her mouth.

"Damn Peggy, I forgot I gave you keys to my house." Ann gathered herself from the bed and wrapped the sheet around her naked body.

"It's cool, don't get up." Peggy waved the gun at Ann.

"Yeah bitch, stay your ass down there." Sherry came from the dark shadows so her face could be seen.

"Sherry, what are you doing here?" Ann was confused.

"I'm fine Robin, how you doing?" Sherry said that as if she was Wendy Williams.

"So, your name is Robin." Peggy asked feeling quite betrayed.

"Wait, I can clear this up." Ann said as she tried to plead her case.

"First, where's Baby D's money and why did you lie and say that I had his money?" Peggy said.

"Baby, put on your pants. Paul, this my best friend Peggy and her sister Kezia. That's Kezia's best friend Pam." Ann felt the need to introduce to each other as she pointed to each girl naming them for Paul.

Peggy looked towards the door, "And this is my sister Sherry."

Sherry walked through the door. The look on Ann's face was priceless.

"Your sister?" Ann screamed as she noticed a familiar face. A face that knew a few of her secrets and rendezvous on how she came across so much money.

Tara stood at the top of the bed. She was leaning so close to the wall that the lamp on the nightstand had blocked Ann's view of her. Tara noticed that Ann began to move around. Tara seen as she began to fumble around the pillows in the bed. She came from the shadows of the nightstand, "Bitch stop reaching for your gun baby!"

Ann shook her head in disbelief. She was so upset with herself. She had been the mastermind behind so many felonious capers that she didn't even see this coming.

"Well hello, Paul, how are you doing?" Tara spoke very seductively.

"Fine lil sister, how are you?" Paul gathered himself and stood to his feet. Ann tried to follow.

Peggy didn't want her to move, "Sit down Ann, I mean Robin. Kezia, go in the basement and get the money out of the safe." Peggy looked into Kezia's direction and then back to Ann, "When were you going to tell me about your house in Texas? Bitch, I looked at you like one of my sisters and bitch you used me?"

"I'm sorry Peggy. I was going to tell you everything." Ann said as she knew this was not going to end good for her.

"Bullshit, whore. You were going to leave and cross me out on everything. But in the next world I hope you find a good friend like me." Peggy moved in for the kill.

"Wait Peggy!" was all she got out. Blood began to squirt as Peggy made the incision on Ann's throat.

"Damn Peggy, you cut her throat like that!" Paul was shocked. He knew his sister was violent but now he was seeing in firsthand.

"Tara, what are you doing?" Pam asked as she watch Tara move things around on Ann's bed.

"Just give me those pillows." Tara was looking for some assistance.

Tara put the pillows over Ann's head and shot twice. "Now stick a fork in that bitch because she's done!"

"Shit JJ should have mad you all the sons in the family." Paul said as he witnessed his other sister pull the trigger on an already dead corpse.

Peggy had been to Ann's house several times. She even had a key. Peggy had forgot all about the key with all the stuff she had on her mind. After she pulled the trigger she ran to Ann's bathroom to gather her thoughts.

Everyone stood over the bed looking at the dead body in silence. No one didn't know what they should do. The brain of the operation had left the room in a hurry. Kezia was getting the money. Pam made the first move and left the room.

She knocked on the bathroom door, "Hey sis, you okay?"

Peggy splashed water on her face and looked in the mirror trying to think of their next move, "I guess so, I mean, how am I supposed to feel, I just killed the girl that I loved like one of my sisters."

The sister part hit a nerve for Pam. She would never go against her girls. She was loyal like that, "Fuck that bitch! The bitch crossed you!" Pam said with force. "That's grounds for death!"

They all gathered in Ann's kitchen. Kezia sat the money on the kitchen table. She began to put the money in stacks of thousands.

Peggy phone began to ring. She looked down not noticing the number she was quite hesitant to answer. The call ended. A few seconds more the phone began to ring. Peggy noticed the unknown number again. Everyone was looking at her wondering why she wasn't answering her phone.

Peggy pressed answer on her phone, "Hello?"

"Is this Peggy?" the stranger on the phone asked.

"Why? Who the fuck is this?" Peggy was pissed because she couldn't recognize the female's voice.

"First, is this Peggy?" the female was very persistent and her tone let Peggy know that this female on the other end wasn't going to stop asking until she confirmed she was Peggy.

"Bitch, who the fuck is this?" Peggy spoke firmly letting her know she wasn't about to give out information.

"My name is Betty. I need to talk to you about Red." The caller said.

Peggy was very offended when she heard her man's name, "Red, what about him?"

"Can we meet somewhere so we can talk? Peggy, it took me three years to make this phone call. We need to talk." The caller's tone went soft. She was on the brink of tears.

Peggy agreed, "Okay. I'll meet you at 3:00 on Mimika."

Betty didn't want that as the meeting place, "Red will see me."

Peggy got an instant attitude. She knew Red only concerned should have been her. She was the only factor that matter at that point and she know Betty needed to know this. Peggy snaked her neck, "So what. I'll see you at 3 pm on Mimika. Betty, don't bullshit me."

Betty agreed to the meeting place and the time, "I'm not."

Peggy stood up and realized it was time for them to leave, "Pam, turn the heat off so her body won't smell too soon. Let's go, Paul. Did anybody see you come in here?"

Paul looked at his sister, "No, I rode here with her. My car is at the house."

"Alright you ride with me and Tara. Kezia, you and Pam and Sherry get the money and meet us at my house." Peggy was ready to leave the scene.

Paul had to come into town. Standing 6'2" and weighing in at 175 pounds with caramel skin with his hair cut short, he had knocked Ann off her game.

The ride to Peggy's house, nobody said a word. They all made it into the house. Paul helped Kezia carry the money in the house. Paul walked over to Peggy.

Peggy looked at her brother. She noticed his look of concern, "Hey Paul, you okay?"

Paul answered, "Fine sis, JJ always said that you were a cold-hearted girl. But sis, I still love you! Peggy I just want you to be careful out here in these streets."

Peggy felt good about her brother being concerned. She smiled and said, "Nigga, you were not thinking about my safety when you were getting your dicked sucked!'

Paul laughed and grabbed his manhood, "Sis that was the best head in the world!"

Pam always thought Paul was fine but she never stepped to him. She looked at Paul, "That's what you think!"

Peggy ignored Pam. She turned to Sherry and Paul, "Well thanks for coming to help us out."

Sherry cut right in, "That's what family is for. But we got to get out of St. Louis, too much for me!"

Peggy told Kezia to give Sherry and Paul their half of the money. Kezia had already separated and divided amongst them. She just needed something to put it in. She went to Peggy's room and retrieved a shoe box.

Peggy knew what she was about to say would make Pam happy, "Pam, will you please take Paul to get his things from the house."

Pam smiled, "I sure will."

Peggy hugged her brother and sister, "Sherry and Paul when you get back home turn in the car. Call me and let me know you all made it safely.

Pam, Paul and Sherry walked out the house. Peggy went to lay down and gather her thoughts. She had to meet the woman that called her. She wondered what this meeting was all about.

Chapter 3

"Kezia, you ready baby!" Joe asked.

Kezia entered the room, "How do I look?"

Kezia had some Baby Phat jeans with a Baby Phat top to match. She also had on some Baby Phat heels with a matching purse. She had long black hair that hung down her back.

"Damn baby, you look so good, I could you eat you!" Joe licked his lips.

"Joe, I'm not getting ready to be sitting around in this club with all those girls in your face, so you better tell them form the jump to keep it moving."

"Baby, it's all about you!" Joe reassured Kezia, "Why you walking like that?"

Kezia looked back at Joe, "Don't play Joe."

Joe started to laugh. Together they left the house and entered Joe's truck. They were at the club in no time.

"Damn this place is packed!" Kezia said as they entered the club.

"Hi, Joe." Pam said meeting them at the door, "Hey, what's up with you girl? Come on y'all, we are in the V.I.P." Pam led the over to the section that was reserved for them.

Peggy watched as Pam led them over to their section. She couldn't wait until they were close. She had something to say to Kezia.

"Girl, why are you walking like that?" Peggy smirked. Everybody started laughing. "Damn man you putting it on her like that?" Peggy continued.

"Peggy, I'm getting you!" Kezia smiled.

"So Joe, man I heard you getting married." Pam said aloud.

"Yeah, in the morning." Joe smiled.

"Well Pam, he asked me to marry him and I couldn't tell this fine specimen of man no." Kezia smiled admiring her ring.

The DJ started playing Tank and everybody got on the dance floor. Then he came back with R. Kelly's 12 play, the floor was packed! As they left the dance floor Joe's ex-girlfriend grabbed his hand.

"Joe, baby what's up?" his ex was in his personal space.

"Back up girl and let me go. Come on Kezia." Joe brushed her off and grabbed Kezia to walk off the dance floor.

Kezia was not about to walk away that easy, "Who the fuck is this bitch?"

Pam couldn't hear because the music was too loud. Kezia's face expression let her know something was not right, "Hold up Baby D, something's not right."

"Joann, move the fuck out of my face!" Joe said to his ex.

"I'm not going anywhere!" Joann tried to stand her ground.

"Like I said who this bitch?" Kezia looked at Joe and then turned to Joann, "Move, whore, didn't he tell you to get the fuck out of his face?"

Joann friends were in eye distance of her. They were watching her every move. When they saw that there were was in the midst they rose to the occasion but it wasn't quick enough. Kezia picked up a beer bottle and slapped Joann in the face with it and Pam pulled out her gun.

Pam flashed her gun, "What you girls want?"

Joe looked at what was going on and felt very uncomfortable, "Damn baby, let's go!"

Pam was amped, "You bitches better know who you stepping to!"

Baby D was impressed. He thought that's how girls from Brooklyn, New York simply got down. He was trying to remember where she pulled the gun from, "Man, you see that?"

Joe had to admit he was just as impressed, "Hell yeah!"

"Red baby, answer your phone!" Peggy screamed from the bathroom.

"Where is Ms. Brown? That's what we pay her for." Red said as he heard the phone ringing.

"Baby that's your private phone." Peggy said.

"Shit, what time is it?" Red went to retrieve the phone.

"12:30." Peggy said.

"Shit, we about to sleep the whole day away." Red rose up from the bed.

The phone continued to ring. Red was getting irritated by the ringing of the phone. He only used it for business. He had turned off his cell phone. He had been getting phone calls from Betty on that phone. Peggy never answered and at that moment he didn't want to answer while Peggy was there. He knew he couldn't keep letting it ring. He snatched the phone up.

"What?" Red held the phone awaiting the moment he was about to slam it down.

"Man, Red you hear the news." JaDarrell said.

"I'm still in bed." Red was relieved.

"They found Peggy's friend, Ann dead!" JaDarrell informed him.

"You bullshitting!" Red couldn't believe what he was hearing.

"For real man." JaDarrell tried to convince him it was real.

"Damn! That's fucked up!" Red was thinking about how he was about to break the news to Peggy. For the past three years they had become thicker than thieves.

"Man I hate to hear that. Where did they find her?" Red asked.

"At her house, somebody killed her, cut her throat." JaDarrell continued.

"Let me tell Peggy. I'll holla at you later." Red hung up the phone and went to locate Peggy. When he found her in a closet on the guest bedroom he called her name, "Peggy?"

"What baby?" Peggy never turned around. She just continued tossing clothes on the bed from the closet.

"Hey can you stop for a second and sit down?" Red tried to hold back the tears.

"For what?" Peggy turned to look at him.

Red began to speak very slowly, "Baby somebody killed your friend Ann."

Peggy paused. She thought to herself for a second. She didn't know how to respond. She sat down on the bed next to the pile of clothes. She looked at Red with tears in her eyes and said, "What Red, you're playing right?"

"Baby, I'm not playing. JaDarrell just called and told me." Red was waiting on a different reaction.

"Where he say it happened" Peggy wanted to know how much did Red actually know.

"Her house." Red didn't get the reaction he expected, "I'm sorry baby."

"Any word on who did it?" Peggy led Red from out the guest room. They were back in their bedroom. She turned on her television.

"No, turn on Channel 2 news." Red said.

"It's the best isn't it, baby?" Peggy said. Just as she turned the channel, the news was reporting the Breaking News. They both sat in silence as the news reporter gave graphic details about the woman that Peggy knew as Ann.

"Damn, nobody seen anything and they burned down her house, that's fucked up! Why they calling her Robin Pipe?" Red looked at Peggy for an answer.

"I don't know." Peggy was trying to figure out who sat the house of fire. When they left the house was still standing.

"Baby, I'm going to take me a shower and hit the block and see what's going on. Peggy, when are you going to ship our stuff out of here?" Red asked.

"Today. The moving company will be here at 4:00. I am gonna have them move those bedroom suites out. I am going to leave everything that's downstairs just like it is so no one knows anything." Peggy said to Red.

"Okay. Call my cell phone as soon as you hear anything." Red was looking for something to put on. He continued to talk to Peggy, "Damn, first Dave and his girlfriend, now Ann. Dave wake is Thursday and his girl Tracey is Sunday. It is time to go." Red walked into the shower.

Peggy went to talk to Mrs. Brown, "I'll be back by four to help you pack up everything in the other six bedrooms and everything in the basement is going to you and your family."

"Oh, Ms. Peggy, thank you so much but I didn't know you all were moving." Mrs. Brown said.

"We're not. What time is it? "Peggy avoided having that conversation with Mrs. Brown. The less information she had the better.

"1:45." Mrs. Brown answered.

"I have to make a run. If anyone calls me, tell them that I'm sleep. I'll be back in one hour. And call your family and tell them that the moving company will be bringing that stuff today." Peggy informed Mrs. Brown. She had already made the arrangements for Mrs. Brown to get the furniture.

"Okay, thank you Ms. Peggy, I'll see you later!" Mrs. Brown said with a big smile showing her missing two front teeth.

Peggy was on her way to meet the chic who called her phone about her man Red. She said aloud to herself, "Who is this girl Betty and what does she need to talk to me about?"

Her thoughts were interrupted when her cell phone began to ring. She fumbled around for it in her purse. She finally grabbed it and pressed answer, "Yeah."

"What's up sis? Well I need to tell you something." Kezia said not sure why she was so afraid to tell Peggy about what she had done.

"What is it?" Peggy said.

"Joe asked me to marry him." Kezia informed her.

"What? Are you crazy?!" Peggy screamed.

"Peggy, I'm not going to lie, I fell in love with him and I married him this morning!" Kezia couldn't even finish her conversation. Peggy had ended the call.

As Peggy dialed Tara she was pissed, "I don't believe this shit!" Peggy listened to Tara's phone ringing. She was hopping that it didn't go to voicemail and Tara would answer. Just as she was about to hang up and try it again she heard Tara answer.

Peggy yelled through the phone, "Tara!"

"Yeah!" Tara said.

"Kezia done lost her damn mind?" Peggy said.

"What are you talking about?" Tara asked as if she didn't already know.

"This bitch married Joe this morning." Peggy informed her of something she knew but she acted as though she was surprised.

"What? You Bullshitting? Where are you at Peggy?" Tara need to switch the conversation.

"Coming down Riverview, going on Mimika to meet some girl name Betty." Peggy told Tara.

"Who is that?" Tara didn't understand why Peggy hadn't said this before.

"I don't know, she called my phone talking, about, she need to talk to me. I'm here now, I'll call you back." Peggy hung up on Tara.

"Damn that nigga Quick is fine and his motherfucking twin brother with those pretty ass eyes and those bow-legs. And they keep them some jobs too. These dumb bitches better get on these niggas." Peggy said to herself as she seen the guys out on the block. She noticed an unfamiliar face. She parked and walked over to the chic she assumed was Betty.

"Hey are you, Betty?" Peggy checked her out.

"Yes, I am Betty."

"I'm Peggy. Come on, we can go in the house and talk. Well what do you want?"

Peggy led her into her family's house. She instructed her to sit and she did.

Betty started right in, "Well I think it's time you know that I have a little girl by Red. She is three years old and her name is Tasha Strong."

Peggy was upset. Someone shared something with her man that she didn't. "So, what the fuck you want me to do? I didn't fuck you. I don't do bitches!"

"I think it's time for Red to start taking care of his child. You and he ride around in new cars and trucks. Dressing like he own the mall."

Peggy was hurt but she was not about to show it. She wasn't about to turn her back on Red. She was curious and needed answers. She needed to know why now, "Why you wait so long to come and just for the record, Red doesn't have any money. So, this money talk is over with. Let me ask you something, Red doesn't take care of your child?"

Betty felt a little ashamed but she answered, "No, he rides right pass like he don't know her. He knows that my daughter is his little girl. She looks just like him. Tasha needs shoes and clothes. She would like to stay in a pretty house with a back yard in a nice area too!"

"Does Tasha want these things or you do?" Peggy didn't know what to think.

Betty was honest, "Both. So, next month, I'm going to take Red to court to make him take care of Tasha."

Peggy didn't want to hear anymore. She was ready to be confrontational but she kept her composure, "You want some money, let me put a bug in your ear. You are not gonna get shit! Because Red don't have shit! And when we go to court, be ready to have a DNA test. Now get the fuck up out of here!"

"I'll see you in court, Ms. Peggy!" Betty exited like she entered.

"I'll be there!" Peggy shouted as Betty walked down the side walk, "Make sure you tell me the date and time."

"November 2nd at 10:30 in the morning, Boo." Betty shouted as she entered her car.

"Like I said, we'll be there and you are not getting shit! Goodbye." Peggy shot back.

Peggy drove like a mad woman. She wanted to call Red to tell him to meet her at the house. She didn't want to take her eyes off the road. She was too busy trying to dry her eyes. She was hurt. This was a pain she couldn't explain. Red had played around. She thought she could deal with certain things. A baby was taking her hurt to a new level. It was as though he entered her soul and just began to walk all over her heart. She was so angry that she was furious. A divided opposition was in her thoughts. Then she thought that she wouldn't let him go that easy. She had too much time invested in that relationship.

As soon as she made it in her house, she dialed Red's cell phone. He didn't answer the first time. Crazy thoughts of him being with Betty filled her mind. She immediately called him back.

Red answered, "Hey baby!"

Peggy didn't want to hear the mushy talk, "Don't hey baby me motherfucker, and get your ass home!"

Red was confused, "Hold up, what's all that talk for?"

"Get home now!" was all Peggy said before she ended the call.

"JaDarrell, something is wrong at home." Red said.

"Let's go Red, what have you done?" JaDarrell asked.

"Man, shut the fuck up!" Red was trying to figure out what could Peggy be so upset about, "I haven't done anything." He tried to plead his case with JaDarrell.

Red had never got home that fast. He was driving so fast JaDarrell put on his seat belt. They entered to the house together. They both noticed Peggy had been crying and she seemed very upset.

"What's up, Peggy?" Red tried to read her face as JaDarrell spoke to Peggy.

"Hey, JaDarrell." Peggy spoke sounding very dry.

"Sorry to hear about, Ann." JaDarrell was fishing, too.

"Yeah, me too, but thanks." Peggy said and turned to face Red, "Now what's up nigga, you want to play games?"

"What are you talking about?" Red was very confused and unaware of what games she was speaking about.

"Betty and your lil girl Tasha." Peggy was straight and to the point.

"Peggy, that child is not mine." Red didn't want to hurt Peggy.

"Nigga, you fucked her raw! Now this bitch taking you to court for money." Peggy tried not to cry.

"What?" Red was not trying to go to court.

"The girl is going to court? On your ass. You want to play me like a bitch on the street!" Peggy was very upset.

"Peggy, baby calm down! Let's talked about this." Red didn't want her upset.

"JaDarrell man, can you go to the back room." Red wanted to be alone with Peggy.

"No, stay there. I have nothing to hide. Call the lawyer right now." Peggy said to Red.

"Lawyer for what?" Red was confused.

"Call him now. Mrs. Brown, Can you get Mr. Jones on the phone for me, thank you." Peggy was not for the games, "Shut up Red. Mr. Jones, is on the phone." Peggy handed him the phone. Then she snatched it back. She decided it would be best for her to do the talking.

"Mr. Jones, how are you doing?" Peggy asked when she heard the lawyer's voice.

"Fine." Mr. Jones replied, "What can I help you with?"

"Mr. Jones, we need you to take Red's name off everything and make it seem that his wasn't on anything at all."

"Ms. Peggy, what's going on?" Mr. Jones asked.

"Some girl name Betty is taking Red to court for child support. She said court is November 2nd. I want you to make it seems like Red never had anything. And he works a little job at my daddy's junk yard. He bring home six hundred dollars a month and he lives with me at my family's house on Schulte. And we want a DNA test." Peggy got that all out in one deep breath.

"And if the little girls turn out to be his?" Mr. Jones asked.

"The Red will pay $125 month. Thank you." Peggy tried to be firm.

"No, problem." Mr. Jones said.

"And Mr. Jones if you pull this off for us, we have a big bonus for you." Peggy said.

"Alright, I'll have all this done in a week." Mr. Jones said.

"NO! I need this done in 72 hours." Peggy said.

"That's pushing it, Peggy." Mr. Jones told her.

Peggy needed this done or she was going with someone else, "Can you do it?"

"I can do it." Mr. Jones told her.

"Alright, thank you." Peggy hung up ending the call.

"Peggy, I'm sorry." Was all Red could muster up. He looked every bit of guilty.

"Red, I now a man is going to be a man but your ass went up in that bitch raw! What the fuck were you thinking? On November 2nd after court, we will get married. Your name will not go anything for a year. I will set up a bank account in the meantime $1000 in it. And every two weeks you put $50 in it and that's all. I will call my daddy and tell him to you up some paycheck stubs for that last two months." Peggy was going to support him rather he was right or wrong. She continued to talk and he just listened, "Friday you will pick up a $300 check from there and cash it at your bank and keep the stubs and give him the money back. You will not hustle until this court shit is over with. Are we on the same page?"

"Yeah, baby." Red sounded as though he had lost his best friend.

"Red, I'm not trying to stop you from being a man but I'm not going to let this whore take our shit, alright baby? And the next time something you do it in the streets comes to our door, we gonna have some big ass problems!" Peggy exited the room. She was done talking about the situation.

Chapter 4

"Peggy, I'm so glad you gonna be my sister-in-law!" JaDarrell smiled like a kid in a toy store as he talked to Peggy.

"Thank you, JaDarrell." Peggy was just as happy considering the circumstance.

"A sister-in-law who can think on point like you, and can hold a nigga down like you!" JaDarrell was impressed on how Peggy was handling his brother's situation.

"Boy, you so crazy!" Peggy blushed.

"Peggy, I'm for real." JaDarrell turned to get his brother and Peggy's attention, "Red and Peggy, I need talk to you both."

"About what?" Red asked.

"Can we sit down?" JaDarrell pointed to the chairs.

"Yeah. What's up lil brother?" Red said as he took his seat.

"Well, Red, man we have a very nice bank account." JaDarrell said as he thought about all the money they had.

"Well, you don't." Peggy pointed to Red. Right now he wasn't entitled to anything that Betty could have access.

Everybody started laughing.

"Shut the hell up!" Red said as he understood the point Peggy was making.

JaDarrell continued with the point he was trying to make, "What I'm saying is I'm ready to find a lady and settle down with and have a family. So, I'm getting ready to leave St. Louis, man, it's time to move on. I know we said we would never leave each other but, man, it's time to go!" JaDarrell was tired with all the death and drama that was taking place in the city.

"Well, JaDarrell, I've been telling Red that, too. I think it's time to show people that there is life after the ghetto!" Peggy said in agreement with the point JaDarrell was trying to make.

"I know that's right. Man we got so much money we cannot spend it all in this lifetime, or the next one. So, after your court stuff is over with and you two get married, I'm out of here." JaDarrell said.

"Where are you going?" Red looked at his brother and waited on him to respond.

"Down south, man I was hoping you would come with me. There's nothing else up here for us all. All of our family members, have left St. Louis five years ago. Man, Peggy and Red, come go with me, I don't want to be by myself!" JaDarrell was trying to convince them both. He was ready to leave he just didn't want to go alone. If push came to shove he was going to leave with or without them.

"JaDarrell, where down south are you trying to go?" Peggy became very interested when he spoke of the south.

"I don't know, I just know that I'm leaving here." JaDarrell was ready for change. This was his cry for help.

"JaDarrell, if you go to Florida, we will go, too!" Peggy said.

"For real sister-in-law!" JaDarrell was so excited he hopped up and hugged Peggy.

"Well, I'm getting ready to look for me a house in Florida and we can't tell people where we're move." Peggy added.

"I don't plan to tell anybody where I'm going." JaDarrell confirmed.

"I'll start looking in the morning for us a house." Peggy said to JaDarrell. She didn't want to tell him that they already had plans to leave.

"Peggy, I know you have a sister, hook me up." JaDarrell said as he knew who he had in mind but he didn't want to say her name.

"I got a real square sister." Peggy told him.

"Hook me up!" JaDarrell said.

"Alright JaDarrell, I'll call her tonight and tell her." Peggy smiled.

"Does she work?" JaDarrell wanted to know if she knew how to get her own or if she just waited on handouts.

"She's a nurse." Peggy said proudly.

"For real?" JaDarrell was slightly impressed.

"Yes, I'm for real. I wouldn't bullshit you with nothing about my family." Peggy said with major confidence.

"What's her name?" Red wanted to know. He had sat and watched this conversation take place as though he was at a tennis match.

"Karen." Peggy kept it brief.

"She doesn't have any kids do she? How does she look? Does she look like you?" JaDarrell said. He was anxious and ready to settle down. He had become quite tired of one night stands and he found it very hard to trust anyone. He knew if he got with one of Peggy's sister he wouldn't have to worry about betrayal. From what he had seen and notice from Peggy's family is they were close and loyal.

He remembered her telling him about her dad J.J. had nineteen kids. Her dad made sure his kids knew each other and had love for each other. J.J. was very nice on the eyes. He was six feet tall and with flawless caramel skin that he had passed on to most of his children. Gray eyes during the day and green eyes during the night. His children had either green or gray eyes. Although, he had several woman he only loved Peggy's mother Robin, who had his first four kids. J.J. may not love the other women as deep as he did Robin, but he cared about all his kids.

"Not to me but everybody say we do." Peggy said to JaDarrell as she thought about how strong her dad genes were.

"Hook me up okay?" JaDarrell continued.

Peggy cell phone rang. She nodded her head to let JaDarrell know that she would take care of it. She listened to the caller and said yes every few seconds.

Red figured this would be a good time to leave, "Come on, JaDarrell, let's ride." He turned to Peggy but not trying to interrupt her call. He spoke softly, "I'll be back in two hours?"

In a split second JaDarrell and Red were gone and Mrs. Brown had entered the kitchen. She noticed that Peggy was on the phone so she didn't disturb her.

"Mrs. Brown, the movers will be here in thirty minutes, is everything ready, is it all packed up? Did you call your family?"

'Yes, they are so happy!" Ms. Brown answered.

"Well call them back and tell them that the men are going to bring the stuff as soon as they get here." Peggy told her.

"Ms. Peggy, do mean the big TV, too?" Mrs. Brown was getting very excited.

"Yes, Mrs. Brown, everything in the basement is yours." Peggy informed her

"Thank you!" Mrs. Brown stated.

"I have to make a call alright." Peggy said to Mrs. Brown. That was her way of saying you need to leave so I can be alone.

Peggy placed a call. She had something on her mind that was bothering her. She waited as the phone began to ring. "Hello, Pam, can you talk?"

"Yes." Pam didn't know if that was a trick question. She wanted to say that was what her mouth was used for but she decided against it. Peggy sounded a little sad.

"Did my sister get married for real?"

"Yes, and Joe is buying a house in New York."

"How did this shit happen?" Peggy had to know because this was not a part of the plan

"You got to see her ring. Everybody at the courthouse was looking at it." Pam was happy for her best friend even if her sister wasn't.

"So how are you and Baby D doing?" Peggy needed to know. The entire part of her plan was to bring Baby D down. His riches were going to help her survive her life after leaving the ghetto.

"Fine, but I'm not getting married! Peggy, Joe really love Kezia! He has put her name on everything he got and they are flying back to New York next week to look for them a house." Pam wasn't trying to take that route. She was happy that her friend was happy.

"Baby D going, too?" Peggy needed confirmation that Baby D demise was still the focus.

"No. Joe, doesn't want anybody to know where he's moving to. Plus, what is Baby D going for?" Pam knew what Peggy was trying to get to. She just wanted her to say it.

"To be with you." Peggy said in a matter of fact tone.

"Peggy, we cool and all but I like Paul." Pam said trying to put Peggy at ease.

"Who?" Peggy couldn't believe what she was hearing.

"Paul, your brother. I like him real hard. I can't stop thinking about him. Peggy, what am I going to do? He didn't even look at me." Pam felt she said enough to let her know that she was not feeling Baby D like that.

"Girls, you so crazy. I am about to call him for you right now and hook this thang up." Peggy said she clicked over. She needed to put Paul in Pam's life so the plan of Baby D would still be on. She didn't need Pam catching any feelings. She was already wondering how this would turn out with Kezia and Joe. "Pam, you there?"

"Yeah." Pam confirmed she was on the phone.

"Hello." An unfamiliar voice had answered the house phone. The only ones that stayed there was Paula, Paul and Sherry. They had inherited the house during their mother's untimely death.

"Where's Paul?" Peggy asked.

"Why?" the unfamiliar voice said in a matter of fact tone.

"Who are you?" Peggy remained calmed. She thought it was Paula playing but it didn't really sound like her. She just didn't want to piss Paula off. She got along with Paul and Sherry just fine. It was Paula who usually had the beef. Paula hated the fact that Peggy was the oldest. She was conceived out of love and Paula felt she was conceived from lust. Her feelings were the truth.

"Mary."

"So, tell him Peggy's on the phone, Mary!"

"Peggy Jean?"

"No, Peggy his sister!"

"Paul, some girl on the phone talking about she your sister name Peggy." Mary yelled to Paul.

"Give me the phone, and why are you answering my phone girl, Go Home! Yeah, sister, what's up?" Paul said firmly.

"Nothing, what's up with you?" Peggy said.

"Nothing, Hey Peggy, I was going to call you today. I needed to ask you something about that girl." Paul said.

"What girl?" Peggy was hoping he was talking about Pam since she was the one on the phone listening.

"Pam." Paul confirmed her feeling.

"What about, Pam?" Peggy asked.

"Is she married or has someone special in her life?" Paul inquired.

"No, but what about Mary?" Peggy was being funny.

"Don't play, I don't like that girl like that." Paul confirmed.

"That's not what she said. She said you are her man." Peggy chuckled.

"What? You bullshitting!" Paul only smashed Mary every now and then. That situation was complicated because Mary was a married woman.

"No, I'm not." Peggy continued to chuckle, "Pam, ain't that what she said?"

"Yeah." Pam played along.

Paul smiled, "What's up, Pam?"

"Nothing." Pam kept it brief but she was glad that Paul had mentioned her.

"Paul the reason I'm calling you is because Pam likes you and wants you to hook up with you." Peggy said.

"For real?" Paul day had been made and shown in his voice, "Pam, is that the truth?"

"Yes." Pam answered.

"Pam, girl I've been thinking about you every day." Paul had to let her know.

"Same here." Pam had to let him know the feelings were mutual.

"You still in St. Louis?" Paul asked knowing she lived in Brooklyn, New York.

"Yes." Pam said not ready to go home.

"Can I call you?" Paul asked.

"Yes." Pam was ready to jump for joy. Paul had been in her thoughts ever since she had taken them to pick up their things before they left to go back to Memphis.

"Paul, you know I had Kezia come down here to take care of some biz right?" Peggy had to tell someone how Kezia had betrayed her.

"Yeah." Paul said.

"This girl went and married the nigga!" Peggy wanted to say more but she decided against it because Pam was still on the phone.

"What?" Paul didn't know what Peggy wanted him to say or do so he kept his statement brief.

"From what I hear, the nigga put her name on everything and he moving to New York, too." Peggy said it as though it was horrific news.

"I'm moving to New York, too. If Pam act right." Paul laughed.

"Damn boy, you haven't gotten the pussy and ready to move." Peggy laughed. Peggy could her Pam laughing as well.

"Stop laughing at my brother, Pam. Paul, don't you still have Pam's cell phone number?" Peggy said as she was ready to end the phone call

"Yeah." Paul said.

"Call her, I got something to do alright?" Peggy said.

"Love you, sis." Paul said as he was about to get off the phone with Peggy and Pam.

"I love you too, bye." Peggy said.

"Pam, I'll talk to you later alright." Paul said to Pam.

Peggy press end on her cell phone. She had just remembered that she needed to call her little sister back. She knew she had probably worried her. She was surprised that Tara hadn't called her to see what was going on with Peggy.

"Tara, what are you doing?"

"Waiting on you to call me back. Who is Betty and what does she want?" Tara said.

"Money. She says that her little girl is by Red."

"What? Did you beat her ass?" Tara wanted to know what had popped off between her sister and this Betty chic.

"No, but I did tell her she's not getting shit! I called our lawyer and took his name off of everything until we got to court." Peggy spoke with major confidence.

"She's taking him to court?" Tara wanted to know what that was all about.

"Yeah." Peggy had Betty's voice on repeat in her mind. She continued to talk to Tara, "November 2nd at 10:30 am, I'm going, too." Peggy had to fill Tara in with the other news she had learned, "Well Kezia did get married, that girl is crazy, she don't know shit about him. Joe put her name on everything and moving to New York with her to buy a house." Peggy spoke with an envious tone.

"Damn lil sis pussy whipped him!" Tara laughed.

Peggy laughed along with Tara. She had more news for Tara, "Pam likes Paul.

"Who? Our brother, Paul?" Tara was taking it all in.

"Yes."

"And Paul likes her, he talking about moving to New York to be with her."

"Peggy, I'm closing on my house next week."

"Good."

"You still moving?" Tara had to ask. Peggy hadn't said anything lately and her house had no signs that she was about to move.

"Yes." Peggy was brief. She didn't know the date or time. Betty had put a monkey wrench in her plans. They could leave and just come back for the court date, but if she needed to be in town until this issue was resolved. She felt she could keep an ear out if she was closer.

Chapter 5

"Peggy, get up, we have to be in court in an hour." Red shook Peggy's sleepy body.

Peggy turned over and spoke with morning breathe, "Red, tell Mrs. Brown to fix some coffee for me and a boiled egg. While I take a shower. Red, take the shit off baby." She noticed him in a nice crisp white Sean John oxford shirt with some gray fresh out of the cleaner's slacks. "You gotta go looking like you don't have any money. You got to go thug looking, no rings. And we are going in the Cutlass alright."

Red changed quickly. He opted for some old jeans and a blue T-shirt that said, I MATTER.

Peggy walked into the kitchen, "Good morning, Mrs. Brown."

"Good morning, here's your coffee and boiled egg" Mrs. Brown placed the items on the table in front of her.

"Thank you Mrs. Brown. I would like for dinner today, some greens, lamb chops, cornbread, spaghetti, and homemade lemon cake, ok?" Peggy looked to see if Mrs. Brown was listening to her instructions.

Mrs. Brown pulled out her little note pad. She used this pad and similar pads to make grocery list, her to do list, take messages or just simple notes. When Peggy seen the notepad, she knew that Mrs. Brown was going to take care of dinner just liked she asked.

The doorbell rang and Mrs. Brown left the kitchen to answer the door.

Tara walked in the kitchen with all smiles. Red followed in right behind her. He was coming for breakfast. He was abnormally nervous. He didn't know what to expect from this court hearing.

"Hello, sis what's up?" Tara said as she entered the kitchen. She turned to speak to Red, "Hi, brother-in-law."

"I still can't believe that you are sisters." Red said thinking about he and Tara incident.

"Well, we are." Tara said in a matter of fact tone.

"We're going in the Cutlass, it look so plain. Your old car doesn't say money at all. You never know who will be watching us pull up. Hell, Betty may be outside trying to take pictures to see if we roll up in one of those trucks." Peggy said to Red.

"Peggy, I see where you are going with this. I understand. You don't have to keep trying to make this we gotta look broke statements. You just make sure you do the same. You can't be looking all fancy. They be wondering what Beyoncé would want with a trash man."

Peggy and Red left to go to the court hearing. Tara went along to be Peggy's support system. As they arrived at the door the Sherriff asked for weapons. Another Sherriff instructed them to place all items, including what they had in their pocket on the conveyer belt.

Red asked the Sheriffs where was court room twenty-three. They pointed down the hall and it was the second door on the left.

Red entered the courtroom and walked up to his lawyer. "Good morning, Mr. Jones." Red said as he shook his lawyer's hand. Mr. Jones then reached to shake Peggy's hand.

"Good morning, how you guys doing?" Mr. Jones spoke to them both.

"Fine." Peggy and Red said in unison followed with a laugh.

"Peggy, are they going to read the DNA test, they did it two weeks ago?" Mr. Jones was preparing Peggy for the results. He had Red come to his office two weeks ago to take the test. He knew Peggy was unaware of this taking place.

As the Sherriff stated for all to rise, their conversation ended abruptly. Once the judge entered and the sheriff instructed everyone to stand. As the judge took his seated he stated, "Everybody be seated."

He then asked what was first on the docket. The court clerk responded, "The State of Missouri vs Quintin Strong." The judge asked was the defendant in court and then ordered Red to approach the bench.

"Good morning, Judge Smith."

"Good morning, Mr. Jones." The judge said very nonchalantly.

"Well judge we are here because Betty Jackson has filed for child support against my client Quintin Strong. Mr. Strong works at a junk yard and after takes, he takes home pay is roughly six hundred dollars a month. They have taken a DNA test two weeks ago and we do not have the results. If it turns out that my client is the father he willing to pay one hundred dollars per month, anything else he will not be able to live. He also agrees to assist with child care. He has family members that is willing to watch the child while the mother works." Mr. Jones said to his longtime friend, Judge Smith.

"Well, let see what the results say. Mr. Strong please step forward. Mr. Strong this is your child and you are here ordered to pay seventy-five dollars a month due on the 15th of every month. Court dismissed." Judge Smith banged his gavel.

Chapter 6

"Thank you, Mr. Jones." Red shook his lawyer's hand.

"Just doing my job Mr. Strong, you need to be thanking Ms. Peggy, girl you got a head on you!" Mr. Jones said.

"Thank you." Peggy said not knowing the judge and the lawyer were longtime friends.

"Red, you son of a bitch! All you gonna give your child is seventy-five dollars a month?" Betty was pissed.

"I am going to provide for my child. All you are gonna get is seventy-five dollars. That's what the judge ordered." Red smiled.

"You can pick her up every weekend." Betty said.

Peggy could no longer stand back quietly. She began to speak, "Now listen to me bitch, you will get your money by the 15th of every month. But there will be no weekend shit! There will be no birthday parties, No Christmas, shit. Look at like this you get your money and a baby not my husband."

"Red, are you gonna let her do your child like this?" Betty looked at him as if he had better shut his bitch up.

"You will have your money by the 15th of the month. Come on baby let's go. Mr. Jones are you coming to see us get married?" Red said. He was already providing for his child and Peggy didn't know about it. He just didn't give Betty the money she wanted. He had to get Peggy away from Betty before she had more stuff to say. He could see the hurt in Betty's eyes. He knew that fire head she gave was probably never be free again.

"When?" Mr. Jones said as he saw something that held his interest.

"Now." Red smiled.

"Is this young lady coming, too?" Mr. Jones asked.

Tara was turned on by the all black Armani suit. She had been checking him out ever since Red had approached him. She didn't need nobody to speak for her. She spoke up firmly, "My name is Tara."

"Nice to meet you, Tara." Mr. Jones said.

"Mr. Jones. That's my little sister." Peggy interjected.

"Are you anything like your sister?" Mr. Jones asked Tara.

"Well, my sister is nice. I'm not as nice as she is." Tara smiled.

"If she's the nice one, I hope I don't ever make you mad!" Mr. Jones laughed.

JaDarrell had meet them on the court steps. He had been watching from the distance. He was supposed to go to court with them but he had over slept. He had heard enough and was confused from what he could hear. He had to approach his brother and find out what was actually going on.

"Red, can I talk to you big brother?" JaDarrell had a grin like he was up to no good.

"Yeah, what's up?" Red step aside.

"Why is Peggy calling that bitch her sister?" JaDarrell looked at Tara with a look that could kill her.

Red took a deep breath, "Tara and me squashed that little beef. Peggy is aware of what transpired between us. It's all over now. That's a thing of the past. I know what you are thinking. They are real sisters. They have the same daddy."

"Tell Peggy that bitch better not shoot you no more." JaDarrell said through tight teeth.

"Shut the fuck up!" Red smiled

"Peggy, there go that nigga Pete and Baby D." Tara pointed in their direction.

"What the fuck are they doing together?" Peggy said as she watched them enter the court building on the other end of where they were standing.

"I don't know, but something is up." Tara said as she watched the two enemies walk into a court building as though they were friends.

"Red, baby I have to check my make-up." Peggy said.

"Hurry up baby. Don't keep your future husband waiting too long!" Red knew she was going to be nosey.

"Tara, you make sure you come back." Mr. Jones said as Tara followed behind her sister.

"I will." Tara blew her new boo a kiss.

"Tara, you call Pam and I will call Kezia alright?" Peggy said.

Tara pulled out her cell phone. She located Kezia name and pressed call.

Kezia answered, "Hello."

"Kezia, can you talk?" Tara asked.

"Yeah."

"Don't show Joe anybody in our family. Something is up. Baby D and Pete are down here in court together." Tara said.

"What are you doing in court?" Kezia wanted to know. She had never seen Pete but she knew he was an enemy of Baby D.

"Well talking right now. They look like they are having a meeting." Tara said as she and Peggy tried to see what was going on between the gentlemen.

"Where is Joe?" Tara asked.

"In the shower." Kezia answered Tara's question looking at the bathroom door.

"Is he going somewhere?" Tara asked because she knew he had being laying low for a while.

"I don't know, but I'm gonna find out." Kezia informed her sister.

"Keep me posted." Tara said.

"Fo'sho." Kezia said.

Peggy told Tara to call Pam. She wanted to know if Pam had still been hanging out with Baby D. She needed to know what had Baby D been up to lately. Tara dialed Pam and handed Peggy the phone.

"Peggy, here Pam is." Tara said.

"Yeah." Pam said wanting to know what was the circumstances that went about for her to receive this call.

"Tara, will tell you what's up." Peggy informed Pam

"Yeah." Pam said as she got the phone back, "What the fuck is going on with Baby D?"

"I don't know. But every time his pone rings now he leaves out the room to talk on it. He used to let me hear what he was saying." Pam informed Tara.

"Pam, I want you to cook him dinner and buy a cake with no icing on it." Tara said.

"No icing?!" Pam wanted to know who was going to eat a cake with no icing.

"Just listen," Tara continued with her instructions, "go buy some caramel and a box of ex-lax, put then in a pot of milk. When the milk get hot, put the caramel in the milk. When the caramel is melted, put the box of ex-lax in with the caramel and let it get thick. Put it on that cake as the icing and let it cool. Put it back in the cake box. Let him eat the cake on his own. When he start having the shits, he's gonna get weak. Don't let him go to a doctor. Keep telling his punk ass that he has the flu for about five to seven days. Keep him with juice and water. Make him eat soup. Keep giving him that cake when you can." Tara said as if she were a mad scientist, "Are you at his house?"

"Yeah, he said he'll be back about five." Pam said trying to stomach the instructions she had just been giving.

"Get on your job, sis." Tara said. Before she let her go she needed to know one thing, "You know where all his money is located?"

"That I do know. We're on some street named Floy in the 5700 block in a white house off the corner. He got about five safes. I have the combinations to four of them." Pam said.

"Call us when you back from the store." Tara said.

Tara and Peggy walked outside. Even though it was November it felt as though it was a spring day in April. The St. Louis weather was bi-polar. One day you needed a coat and the next day you could have on shorts.

"Peggy, what took you so long?" Red asked.

"I'm sorry baby." Peggy apologized.

The individuals left one court building heading to another building. Thirty-five minutes later they were married.

"Well how do feel Mrs. Peggy Strong?" Red asked his wife.

"Fine, baby." Peggy was smiling from ear to ear.

"Well Tara, can I take you to dinner tonight?" Mr. Jones asked.

"Sure, what time do you get off?" Tara asked.

"Now, I'm through for the day. We can hang out the rest of the day." Mr. Jones had to let her know he was his own boss.

"Sure. Where do you live?" Tara didn't waste no time.

"In St. Peters." Mr. Jones informed her.

"Let's go to your house," Tara said, "First, are you married?"

"No, I am not married. I don't have any kids before you ask." Mr. Jones said.

"Well. Let's go." Tara walked off so that he could follow.

"You'll come over to our house for dinner ok, 7:30." Peggy said not sure if she was really going to show up since she had just become occupied.

"That's cool." Tara said.

"Tara, I have something to show you alright." Peggy needed to make sure she would show up.

"7:30 it is." Tara agreed.

"Let's go JaDarrell to our house man, we need to talk." Red said to his brother.

"I'm right behind you." JaDarrell said as he followed his brother.

Mr. Jones stayed about forty-five minutes from downtown St. Louis. He and Tara had talked about just about everything. They were pulling into his driveway and she hadn't even paid attention to what part of town he had taken her.

"Well, Tara this is my house." Mr. Jones said as he exited is car.

"You have a very nice house!" Tara said as she got out the car.

"Tara, call me Joseph."

"Your name is Joseph Jones."

"Yes."

They had entered his beautiful home. Tara admired everything as she followed him through the house.

"Would you like something to drink?" Joseph asked.

"No, but I would like to make love to you!" Tara said seductively.

"Tara, are you sure?"

"Yes."

"Tara you feel so good, ride this dick girl! Oh shit this pussy is the best."

"I know daddy, call my name."

"Tara, oh Tara I love you."

"Baby not yet, but you will."

"Who dick is this?"

"Yours, Miss Tara."

"And who else can ride this dick?"

"Just you. Tara, can I taste your juice?"

"Sure daddy."

So Tara climbed on his face and rode it like she was the Lone Ranger was riding Silver.

"I'm coming daddy, eat all my sweet juice baby. Give me a kiss."

As they were kissing, Tara leaned over his chair so Joseph could hit her from the back. Joseph's dick was so big it could fill up three pussies and still have some for Tara.

"Oh baby, you pulling my insides down." Tara moaned.

"This is my pussy."

"Yeah."

"I better not hear another motherfucker being in my shit." Joseph said aggressively.

"Oh, daddy it's yours!"

Tara straddled him. She was on top of Joseph enjoying the ride, "Daddy, just you daddy. You are hurting me!"

"This pussy better than gold baby." Joseph was enjoying the wetness.

About an hour later Joseph started hollering, "Here it comes baby! I'm coming baby!" He came so much, felt like he could fill up a tub.

"You okay?" Joseph asked.

"No." Tara said.

"Don't be like that baby. Tara, I mean every word I said. I don't do one night stands. You belong to me now."

"I don't belong to any motherfucking body!"

Joseph walked up to Tara and held her head up, "Look at me. You are my lady now. Not my woman, not my wifey, my lady. So, tell all those other dudes you talking to it's over. Come on baby, let's get in the hot tub."

"Joseph, I can't walk."

"Damn baby, I worked the shit out my pussy."

"I'm telling you now. You need to throw your little black book away." Tara said thinking about the other women that he may have in his life.

"My little black book was thrown away when I laid eyes on you."

"Mrs. Brown, did you get everything for dinner?" Peggy asked.

"Yes, Mrs. Peggy, my family loves everything, thank you from all of us."

"Mrs. Brown, we will be having company for dinner, it will be a total of six of us, okay. Oh by the way Mrs. Brown, Red and I got married today." Peggy said.

"What? I'm so happy for you!" Mrs. Brown walked over to give her boss a huge hug.

"Thank you." Peggy said.

Red and JaDarrell were sitting in the family room. They had put in Red's favorite movie. As they were watching *Set It Off* Red thought about what he had saw at court earlier.

"Red, man did you see Baby D and Pete together at court?" JaDarrell said.

"Yeah I saw them but they didn't see me." Red said.

Chapter 7

"Man, the word on the street is that Baby D is going to put down the cross on, Joe." JaDarrell informed his sister-in-law.

"What?" Peggy was shocked.

"Hell yeah, everybody was gambling on Schulte last night, the Lucille boys asked where was Joe and Baby D said that stupid nigga fell in love with some pussy and got married." JaDarrell continued.

"You bullshitting?" Peggy was fucked up behind what JaDarrell just told her.

"That's the word on the street and you know them little niggas is not gonna lie on his punk ass. The word is that Joe is going to pick up six keys, but Joe doesn't know it's a setup!" JaDarrell just continued.

"What! Fuck all this shit, give me my cell phone." Peggy said.

"What's wrong?" JaDarrell said.

"Joe, married my little sister Kezia, what he doesn't know is that we are sisters." Peggy informed her brother-in-law as she dialed her sister.

"Hey sis, can you talk?" Peggy said once Kezia had said hello.

"No." Kezia was brief.

"Well just listen. Is Joe going to do a pick up?" Peggy said.

"Yes, for Baby D, why?" Kezia whispered.

"Don't let him go! It's a setup."

"What?"

"They gonna have the police there." Peggy said not really sure how the setup was going to take place.

"Baby D been acting funny with Joe. Joe called him today and he said that he's gone out of town to visit family." Kezia said.

"He's a damn lie." Peggy said.

"That's why Joe needs to go and do the pick-up because he had a family emergency." Kezia said to her sister.

"Yeah he supposed to pick up six keys. Listen, Joe is family now. When is Joe going to do this?" Peggy asked.

"Tonight at 12 midnight on Lotus and Goodfellow." Kezia knew that Peggy wouldn't lie to her and she figured it had to be some truth to it. She knew about the six keys and she hadn't said anything about it.

"Well Kezia, we got to meet now, you and Joe meet me at my house in thirty minutes, don't tell him anything."

Peggy called Tara. It was time for everyone to get to her home. They were coming for dinner but the matter at hand was more important.

Peggy called Tara. Tara didn't answer. She called her back. Before Peggy could get a word out Tara hollered through the phone, "Peggy, I'm at your door."

Peggy told JaDarrell to open the door for Tara. He did just that.

"Peggy, what's wrong?" Tara asked. She knew that something had to be wrong. Peggy never called like that unless it was.

"I knew my brother-in-law walking into a setup by that scandalous ass Baby D and Pete?" Peggy said.

"Joseph, you know everybody." Tara said, "We're on the first name basis now?"

JaDarrell looked around the room. Tara and his brother's lawyer were booed up. He was just told that Peggy's sister, Kezia, was with Joe. Pam was messing with Baby D. It was as though everybody had someone. He spoke up, "Everybody got somebody except me, that's fucked up."

The doorbell ranged and interrupted what he was about to say. Peggy just went to open the door. She didn't tell JaDarrell she had called her sister for him. It was going to be a surprise.

Karen entered the room. JaDarrell was trying to figure out who she was.

"Hey little sister, you looking good." Tara said.

"Thanks, Tara you, too." Karen said to her family.

"Everybody, this my sister Karen. This JaDarrell, I told you about him." Peggy said as she introduced Karen to JaDarrell.

"Hello, JaDarrell." Karen smiled.

"Hi Karen, nice to meet you. How are you?" JaDarrell said with the biggest smile on his face.

"Doing fine." Karen said as everyone watch what going on between the two.

"That you are! Those your real eyes?" JaDarrell was making conversation.

"Yes, they are." Karen said.

"They are pretty, what color are they?" JaDarrell asked.

"Greenish-gray." Karen said.

"Well, Tara and I, will be back. Mrs. Brown, this is my sister Karen. Show her to the guest bedroom. We gonna be back in one hour." Peggy said as they were rushing out the door.

"Peggy, what are going to do?" Tara asked.

"Help our brother-in-law. Call Pam." Peggy said.

"Shit, this her calling now." Tara said looking at the phone.

"Yeah, Peggy listen, something is going on, and Baby D is going to set Joe up." Pam said.

"I know. Have you even taken Baby D to the house?" Peggy asked.

"Hell no!" Pam yelled.

"Get home, get all of your stuff, and get out of there!" Peggy instructed her.

"I already did. I'm on my way home now." Pam said.

"Put your things up and meet me at my house okay." Peggy said.

"Peggy there is Kezia's car right there. Her and Joe eating at the snack bar, come on." Tara said.

They walked into the snack bar and caught Joe all off guard.

"Well, hello, Joe." Peggy said.

"What's up? Peggy, this is my wife Kezia." Joe said proudly.

"I know Joe, let's talk." Peggy said.

"Talk about what?" Joe asked.

"Joe, what kind of games are you and Baby D are playing with Pete?" Peggy asked.

"What the fuck are you talking about? I don't fuck with Pete and Baby D don't fuck with him any kind of way." Joe said.

"Well, why were they at court together today?" Peggy asked.

"Bullshit! Baby D out of town!" Joe said in a matter of fact tone.

"NO, they were together at court, here look at this." Peggy showed him the picture she had taken with her cell phone.

"That nigga told me he was out of town." Joe was pissed.

"Joe, you are being setup. You are going to pick up for Baby D and the police will be there." Peggy said.

"But, why?" Joe didn't understand why his friend wanted to betray him.

"He said your stupid ass fell in love with some pussy and got married." Peggy said as she repeated what JaDarrell said to her.

"I don't understand this shit." Joe was all confused.

Peggy decided to call JaDarrell so he could confirm what she was saying.

"Hey, JaDarrell. I got Joe right here. I need you to tell him what you know about Baby D."

"What's up, Joe?"

"Man, you got it."

"Man, let us talk to you for minute." JaDarrell said.

"You got my ear for a minute?" Joe agreed.

"Yeah. Yo homeboy hating on you big time. He like yo dumb ass done got some tight pussy and you done fell in love and married the hoe."

"Straight up." Joe just listened.

"When we saw Baby D nigga two nights ago, we were all gambling, that nigga Quick hit him for $6,500, that nigga knows he's lucky. Listen man, word on the street is the Baby D is setting you up for the fall man, tonight. So keep that under your hat." JaDarrell said.

"Check this out lil man, where did you hear that from?" Joe didn't know what to believe. JaDarrell wasn't a friend.

JaDarrell continued, "Those niggas that work for Pete. They were talking about Pete and Baby D hooking up together. They're both over there now on Emma gambling."

"Who?" Joe asked.

"Baby D and Pete. Everybody, I just won four grand." JaDarrell said.

"Good looking out bro." Joe said as he handed the phone back to Peggy.

Chapter 8

"Peggy, good looking out. This nigga told me he was out of town with his family." Joe turned to Kezia, "Thanks baby for making me come to the mall with you. I would have never run into Peggy and the Emma click. I'm killing this nigga and Pete too! Thanks Peggy I owe you. If it's anything you need, just tell me or my wife, but we are leaving town."

"Joe, we need to talk to baby. Joe, you know that I love you right?" Kezia said as she looked into his eyes.

"I hope so." Joe said.

"Well, I do have something to tell you that I never said to you. I just want you to promise this will not change anything." Kezia didn't give Joe a chance to speak. She continued, "Peggy and Tara are my sisters. We have the same dad!" Kezia said in one breath.

"What!? Baby you are bullshitting right?" Joe was shocked. Sleeping with the enemy's family was all he could think. He kept his composure.

"No. Joe, that's why as soon as I heard about the setup I had to get to you out the house to meet Peggy, because we are family now." Kezia said.

"She kept a secret from us. We didn't know you two were married." Peggy tried to reassure Joe.

"Kezia and I will be leaving today." Joe said.

"What about Baby D and Pete?" Peggy wanted to know his plan because she was down with bringing him down.

"You are my sister-in-law's now, we're going hit Baby D where it hurts. Let's go buy three big suitcases." Joe said to the girls.

They walked to JCPenny and bought three suitcases before heading back to their cars.

"Now wait, let me call this nigga." Joe called Baby D.

Baby D picked up as though things were all good when he seen Joe's name flash across the screen, "Joe, what's up?"

"I'm seeing if everything's setup?" Joe asked.

"Everything's cool." Joe informed him, "I'll be back in three days. I'm chilling with the family."

"I now that's right!" Joe could sense the fakeness through the phone.

"Well man I'll holler when I get back alright." Baby D said.

"Later!" Joe ended the call, "Y'all follow me."

They exited the mall. Peggy seen where Joe and Kezia was parked. She drove her car over to where they were. He led them to the highway. Peggy followed Joe without any problem.

"Joe, why are we in the hood?" Kezia asked. He had never brought her to this part of the town.

Joe took them right into one of the cash spots that he and Baby D kept their money. They all opened up the suitcases they had bought and filled them with the dope and cash. Joe moved quickly and calmly. As the girls were filling the suitcases, Joe began to douse gasoline throughout the house. As Soon as the girls made it to the car. He gave them time to put the suitcases in the car. He was looking around to make sure no one had saw him. Joe light a match and ran to the car. As they made it down the street, a loud boom had startled them all. They looked back and all they could see was ruble where the house once stood.

Peggy called Pam. She told her she needed to get everything she had that she wanted from Baby D's house. She instructed her to take all the money that she knew he had in the house. She also told her to clean up and wipe things down.

"No one should know you were ever there. You need to make it look like you never existed. "Peggy told Pam before she hung up the phone she let her know they were on their way there.

Joe and Kezia had got caught at the light. Peggy never looked back to see if they were still behind her. Kezia gave him instructions on where to go. Joe couldn't believe that Baby D had Pam at a spot that he didn't know about.

"Right here, Joe." Kezia pointed out to him where he should par.

"Here Pam, get this bag." Peggy said.

"Shut the door Joe, Shit the money." Kezia said as she thought about the money in the car.

"Now this nigga wants to play the cross game now he broke. This is like six millions dollars. Each one of you take a million apiece. Pam you get yours and the rest is mine and Kezia. Pam, go pack up all your clothes and let's hit the road." Peggy was being the big sister like always.

Joe cell phone began to ring. Joe looked down. He noticed Baby D name come across the screen, "Everyone shut up its Baby D."

"Yeah, man?" Joe spoke calmly.

"Joe, get the fuck over to the house on Floy!" Baby D yelled hysterically.

"For what man?" Joe said all calm and cool.

"Somebody got all our shit!" Baby D said frantically and all out of breath.

"What?" Joe asked trying to play it off.

"They said the house got burned down." Baby D.

Joe paused. He thought to himself, "If the motherfucker burned down, just what was he supposed to be going to get. Then he thought about the safes. They were fire proof." He need to go move the safes.

"Shit, I'm on my way man to check that shit out." Joe said. Then he thought, how did he find out so fast if he were out of town. Inquiring minds needed to know, "Who told you that?"

"Fuck that! Man, Pete called me and told me." Baby D was pissed.

"Who, you breaking up man!" Joe was like no this nigga just didn't say Pete.

"Mike, called and told me." Baby D realized what he had said.

"I'm leaving now." Joe said and ended the call. "Pam you through?" he called out.

"Yes." Pam answered Joe as she noticed his smile had turned to a frown.

"That nigga just let Pete's name come out of his mouth." Joe said.

"Joe, you're bullshitting?" Peggy asked.

"No, I'm not!" Joe said. He knew it was best for him to leave town. He asked the girls, "Where you all heading?"

"Down south." Peggy told Joe. She then turned to Pam and said, "Call Paul and tell him we are on our way."

"Hey, we all will meet up in two weeks, let's go hit the highway." Pam said. She thought about them being in the same rental cars since they had been in town, "We will turn those cars in down there."

"Let me go home. I have been gone for three hours." Peggy said to Tara.

"Well, we're here now. Red, we're back." Peggy said as she entered the house like she had not committed no crimes.

"Tara, come here." Joseph called out.

"What Joseph?" Tara said wit ease.

"I've been waiting three hours here for you." Joseph said.

"I'm sorry baby. I didn't know it was going to take so long. We will talk about it at home alright Joseph?" Tara sneaked in a feel.

"Red and JaDarrell are in the room talking to Peggy. Karen talking to J.J." Tara said.

"Stop calling him J. J. he's our daddy." Karen said.

"So, you came to meet JaDarrell, why?" Tara asked.

"Tara, I came to see everybody." Karen said.

Peggy entered the room with a smile. She yelled towards the kitchen, "Mrs. Brown, you can set the table."

"Okay." Mrs. Brown said.

"Let's eat everybody." Peggy instructed her family.

"Karen, baby would you like some more food?" JaDarrell asked as he was about to wine and dine her at Peggy's expense.

"No, thank you, JaDarrell." Karen said.

"Well let's go in the living room. Anybody like something to drink?" Red said.

"Gin and juice for me!" Joseph said.

"For me, too!" JaDarrell said.

"Peggy and Karen?" Red asked because they hadn't made a choice.

"Quintin, do you or Peggy mind if I step in your den?" Joseph asked.

"It's cool." Peggy said.

"Come here, Tara."

"What Joseph?"

"Don't leave me no more like you did. Red and JaDarrell told me what was going on. Do I make myself clear, do you know how worried I was thinking something was going to happen to you? Baby, please don't do that again." Joseph said with tears almost in his eyes.

"Alright, Joseph Jones!" Tara said.

"So, JaDarrell, how do you like my sister?" Peggy asked.

"That's gonna be my wife!" JaDarrell said.

"Peggy, call and check on Kezia and them, alright?" Red said.

"Hey, Pam how are you all doing?" Peggy asked.

Pam let her know that they had an hour left on the road and she would call her back when they got settled.

Chapter 9

"Hey everybody, we need to talk. We got to leave St. Louis for a while very soon." Peggy said, "All this shit going on, we need to pack up and leave. Our house goes on the market first thing in the morning and the movers will be here at seven in the morning. Wait a minute. Mrs. Brown, I'm giving you our living room set and the bedroom suite and everything in the dining room, and the guest room."

"Oh, Mrs. Peggy thank you." Mrs. Brown said. She was thankful for the stuff that she had given her at first. She now had things she could give to more of her family members.

"So, you call your family and tell them to clean the rooms out where you want the stuff to go. And call you sister and tell her that she can have everything in the den." Peggy said. Paranoia had kicked in and she was ready to go.

"I'll call her right now." Mrs. Brown said leaving the room.

"JaDarrell, what are you gonna do?" Peggy asked her brother-in-law because it seemed he had moved and didn't tell anyone.

"This family on Plover just got burned out. They have a new house and nothing to put in it. I'm going to give everything to them. My clothes and shit is already packed and out of the house. Let me call the family now. "JaDarrell grabbed his phone and scrolled to the family's name. He had got the number from one of the kids and was going to eventually reach out, "Hello, Mrs. Dutch."

"Yes," Mrs. Dutch answered.

"How are you doing?"

"Fine."

"This is JaDarrell."

"Hi son, how are you?"

"Fine."

"Mrs. Dutch, I called to tell you that I'm moving and I left a key for you all in the mailbox to get everything out of the house for your family and your new house. There is two thousand dollars in the drawer for you bills to help you get back on your feet."

"Thank you son, can we go in the morning?"

"Sure, I will call you back in a few days alright?"

"Thank you, bye."

"Damn, when this going down?" Red asked all confused.

"Today!" Peggy said.

"Peggy, did you tell Mrs. Brown about the car?" Red asked.

"I forgot. The Cutlass and the Regal?" Peggy got clarification that Red was giving her both of the cars he had. They were a part of him. He purchased those cars when he first started hustling. He keep them up. They both had new motors, transmissions, fresh paint jobs and brand new tires. The possessed an original new. Mrs. Brown was getting brand new cars.

"Mrs. Brown?" Peggy called out.

"Yes?" she answered.

"What's your daughter's name that goes to college?" Peggy asked.

"Marie, is something wrong?" Mrs. Brown inquired.

"No, Mr. Red is giving her that blue Regal." Peggy told her.

"The car?" Mrs. Brown needed clarification.

"Yes, and the red Cutlass goes to you." Peggy said.

"Thank you Mrs. Peggy! Are you moving?" Mrs. Brown said.

"Yes. Stop crying Mrs. Brown."

"I'm going to miss you and Mr. Red."

"We are gonna miss you too. Is Marie at home?"

"Yes."

"Can Red take her the car now?"

"Yes, I will call her."

"Here are the keys and Mrs. Brown, we are going to pay your salary up to a year. That should hold you until you find another job."

"Thank you, I love the both of you!" Mrs. Brown hugged Peggy tightly.

"Did you call your sister?" Peggy asked Mrs. Brown.

"Yes, she's so happy."

"Okay."

Peggy had brought Red up to speed on everything that had taken place. From Ann to burning down Baby D's stash house. Red was appalled. The streets were talking but they were not saying Peggy was behind it. He let her know that it was best if they went to a hotel. They needed to be hard to find. Red let Peggy know that he had to contact his lawyer to make sure his business matters were squared away. Peggy let him know that they could just go to his house because she needed to see her sister anyway.

The drive to Joseph's house was quiet. Red was letting all the news that Peggy had shared with him sink in. He wondered who he had been sleeping with all this time. He knew that she loved him. He realized that betraying Peggy led to death and vowed never to betray her again.

"Joseph, we cannot let you get in this bullshit!" Red said to his lawyer.

"If Tara is in it, then I'm in." Joseph said.

"Damn, Tara, what you got in your pussy?"

"Shut up, Peggy!" Tara pushed her sister in her arm.

"What about your clothes?" Peggy asked.

Everything!

"I have what I'm going to take with me. I'm going on a shopping spree when I get where I'm going. It's a new start. That city doesn't need to see what this city seen me in." Tara said.

"Nice house, Joseph." Red said as he looked around. He knew his dirty money had help get some of the things in the house he was standing in. He had never called him Joseph until this day. It had always been Mr. Jones.

"Make yourself at home. Sweetheart, show them the bedrooms so they can pick which one they want." Joseph said to Tara.

"They already did. Now let's get down to biz. Red, you need to take care of Pete. Now Baby D is broke, we get Pete first. Let's get Pam on the phone and see if Baby D called her, use the speakerphone." Joseph said to Peggy and Red.

Peggy called Pam, "Hello Pam." Peggy paused because she was trying to make out the sounds that she was hearing. She figured if what she thought was going on, why Pam would answer her phone, "Yeah what's up?"

"I'm fucking if you don't mind." Pam said.

"Well, get up." Peggy shrugged her shoulders not knowing what really to say.

"Hell no Peggy just five more minutes, I'll call back. OH shit Paul." Pam tried to whisper.

"The girl thinks she hung the phone up." Peggy laughed as everyone heard what was taking place.

Pam was moaning so loud. It sounded as though she was satisfying herself. She spoke loudly through the speaker on Peggy's phone, "Paul, baby it feels so good!"

Then Paul finally spoke, "Pam slow down before you make me nut girl!"

"Paul, baby can I ride your dick?"

"Damn Pam, I'm getting ready to nut!"

"Me too!"

"Baby, shit! I love your pussy girl!"

"Paul, that was so good, I got to call Peggy back."

"Hurry up so we can finish." Paul slapped Pam on her butt.

"Peggy?" Pam said as she noticed that her phone hadn't been hung up.

"Yeah, next time hang up your phone. My little brother had you about to cry!'

"Oh shit Paul they heard us." Pam put the pillow on her face to hide her embarrassment.

"Pam, where is Kezia and Joe?" Peggy asked.

"In their hotel room." Pam informed her.

"Pam, have Baby D called you?" Peggy asked.

"Two times!" Pam said.

"What did he say?" Peggy asked.

"Where I am and why I am not at home? Have I talked to Kezia? I told him I was at the mall and I talked to Kezia earlier. And he asked me what did she say and I told him Kezia said she had to go somewhere with Joe tonight about twelve o'clock. Then he asked me was Kezia going with Joe? I told him yeah. And then he started laughing a little and said that is cool. Then he called back to say that he's ready to eat dinner and I'm still at the fucking mall!"

Peggy clicked over to put Kezia on the line. She felt that everybody needed to be clear on what was going on.

"Kezia, has he called Joe?" Peggy asked.

"Yeah." Kezia said.

"Where is Joe?" Peggy asked.

"I'm here." Joe answered. Kezia had already had her speaker on.

"What did he say?" Peggy asked.

"He had to tell me that somebody fucking blowing our spot up and got our shit. I asked him what's the word on the streets, and then he let me know that nobody has seen anything. I told the nigga I'm going to use my money to make the pickup, he said, that's cool. The nigga still playing the cross game!" Joe said as he shook his head.

Chapter 10

"We need to get Pete and then we can get Baby D later. You know where Pete lives, right?" Peggy asked Joe while Kezia had her speakerphone on.

"On the south side on Miami, the house right on the corner!" Joe said.

"But he goes with a girl name Joyce that lives on Ridge. He always at Club Reno and always get there bout 11:30 or 12. When he leave the club, he goes and check his traps on Era every night." Peggy said as she thought about seeing him a few nights when she went to stalk Red down on Mimika.

"Don't you and my sister make a baby!" Peggy said.

"Bye Peggy." Kezia pressed end on her cellphone.

"Joe, Peggy's right use a rubber!" Kezia said to Joe.

"Fuck that shit!" Joe said to Kezia.

"So, baby don't ask me because you know I want kids." Kezia said to Joe.

Peggy turned to Tara. She knew what needed to be done and it needed to be done now, "Let's ride down on Pete tonight." Peggy said to Tara.

A cellphone began to rain. They both looked down. Peggy noticed that it wasn't her phone. "Tara, that's your phone!"

Tara looked at the name as it came across her screen, "its April." Tara answered her cellphone, "Hey girl what's up?"

"Let's go to the club. I need to get out. I haven't been out in a long time." April said to Tara.

"April, I'm not St. Louis, I'm in the ATL." Tara said.

"When did you go down there?" April asked.

"Three days ago, my mother is sick." Tara said.

"When will you be back?" April asked.

"In two more weeks and I'll be home." Tara said.

"Shit Tara, kick it for me!" April said.

"I can't go out, my mother's sick." Tara said.

"Well, I hope she get better." April said.

Tara and April said their goodbyes. Tara let April know that she would call her as soon as she made it back in town. April told her she was going to call another friend because she needed to get out the house. She didn't really want to go to a club but she just needed some fresh air. Tara told her to have fun.

Meanwhile, Red and JaDarrell were on the streets trying to locate Pete. They had been driving through the city trying to find him. They were having no luck trying to accomplish their task.

Tara and Peggy made it back to the hotel. They looked and noticed that Karen had her bags packed and was ready to go. Tara and Peggy looked at each other trying to figure out what was going on.

Peggy asked Karen, "Where is JaDarrell?"

Karen looked at Tara. Then she put her eyes on Peggy and started crying, "I don't know where he is. I just know he left with Red. What I do know is that I am leaving here at 5:45 and going back home. I told my job that I had some family business to take care of but I'm not going to get killed for nobody. Nobody will be calling my job to inform them of my death."

"Karen, you told me you have three weeks off, you haven't even been here a whole week!" Peggy said.

Karen looked at her sisters, "My plane leaves at six a.m."

"Going where?" Tara asked.

"I'm going home." Karen said in a matter of a fact tone.

Peggy looked at her sisters, "Hey I have an idea. Why don't we all take a vacation? We can all go to New York for two weeks."

Tara looked out the hotel window and noticed that Joseph car wasn't on the parking lot.

"Where is Joseph?" Peggy asked.

"He's pulling up now." Tara said as she waited for him to come to the room.

"Joseph, where have you been?" Tara asked.

"To get everybody a plane ticket." Joseph said.

Red and JaDarrell had rode around so long that had burned an entire tank of gas. They headed to the gas station. JaDarrell went in to pay for the gas. He grabbed two orange juices and head back to the car. Red pumped the gas. Once the tank was full they continued their mission. They rode pass an alley and JaDarrell thought he seen Pete's car.

JaDarrell reached over and put his hand on Red's chest, "Hey, bro, bag back." He was right. He could see his head leaned back on the seat and a head bobbing up and down, "Red, there's that nigga in the alley getting his dick sucked."

Red got out his car and tapped on Pete's driver's window. He told the girl to get out the car. She hopped out the car and ran down the alley never looking back. Before Pete could reached his strap, Red had put two in his chest. He ran back and hopped back in the car with JaDarrell.

JaDarrell told Red to pull over when he seen a sewer. He was going to throw the gun down the sewer. Red let him know he was against. The gun belong to Baby D. He didn't know if it was clean or dirty. He just knew it came from one of his spots. Red told JaDarrell just dump and let Baby D catch that case.

"Alright, let's ride. Here come Red and JaDarrell." Tara said as she sat in the hotel window.

"Its 4:55 a.m. Where you been?" Peggy asked Red as he walked up to the door.

"Pete gone!" was all Red said.

"My planes leaves at 6:00." Karen said to JaDarrell.

"Call Pam and Kezia. Tell them to catch a plane to New York tonight." Peggy said.

Tara called the girls like Peggy said.

"Pam, check this out, everybody going to New York for two weeks. You, Kezia and Joe meet us there. Where is Paul?" Tara said.

"Right here sleep." Pam said.

"And girl, stop whipping that pussy on my brother! Put him on the phone." Tara said.

"Paul, Peggy needs talk to you." Tara said.

"Peggy, what's up?" Paul said.

"Shit, getting ready to go crazy in this camp." Paul said.

"So, pack up some clothes for about two weeks, you and Pam and meet us in New York." Peggy said.

"What? New York?" Paul said.

"Nigga, don't you have some money?" Peggy asked.

"Hell yeah! And Pam got about two million dollars." Paul said.

"So, what's the problem?" Peggy asked.

"Shit, flying." Paul said.

"Pam, get up and call from the house phone baby and get our plan tickets." Paul said to Pam.

"When is everybody leaving?" Pam asked.

Pam made the call and found that they had three hours before their flight. They needed to get to the airport an hour ahead a time to make it through TSA.

"Sis, we will be there, we need to talk about Sherry." Paul said to Peggy.

"What about Sherry?" Peggy asked.

"Not on the phone. " Paul said.

Kezia walked into the room to talk to Pam. When she seen Paul on the phone she turned and said to Pam, "I got to call Peggy."

"Paul, is talking to her now." Pam informed Kezia.

Kezia walked up to her brother, "Can I speak to her?"

"Yeah." Paul held his finger up to Kezia telling her to give him a second. He then said to Peggy, "Kezia, wants to talk to you."

Paul handed Kezia the phone.

"What's up sis?" Kezia said to Peggy.

"Did Paul fill you in on our plan?" Peggy said.

"No, Paul didn't say anything. Pam just said something about a vacation. She didn't say too much." Kezia said to Peggy.

"Are you walking around with all that money on you?" Peggy asked.

"Are you crazy, we put that shit in a bank in a safe deposit box? And I opened my own account that Joe doesn't even know about. I put five grand in there." Kezia said.

"I know that's right little sis. I leave in forty-five minutes. I'll see you then." Peggy said.

Peggy and her family head to the airport. They made it to the terminal with no problem. The TSA search was fast and simple. They started walking to their boarding gate. It was not far from the entrance. People had already started boarding the plane.

"Everybody, Kezia will be there, their plane leaves in four hours. We can get their hotel room for them and call them with the hotel we all will be staying in. Tara, who that man, that keeps looking at you?" Peggy said.

"He said his name is Mike. He keeps trying to holler at me." Tara said.

"Girl, Joseph is going to fuck you up and that nigga!" Peggy said.

"Peggy, Joseph got too much thug in him." Tara laughed.

"Tara, he grew up on Grape, took his dope money and went to school to become a lawyer. He went to school with us. Do you remember the boy who use to pull your hair? He also, always asked you to be his girlfriend." Peggy tried to help Tara remember who Joseph was.

"The boy with holes in his shoes, who we called Soft Feet." Tara said.

"Yeah." Peggy said.

"That's Joseph, you is a damn lie!" Tara said remembering the little dirty boy from school.

"Yes, it is. I showed Joseph the game and he took it from there. Saved his money and went to law school. Why do you think he be on you so hard?" Peggy said.

"Here he comes." Tara said slightly embarrassed.

"Peggy, this my seat." Joseph said.

"I know Soft Feet!" Peggy laughed.

"Don't play Peggy, Tara started that bullshit in school." Joseph said.

"So Joseph, you are that boy that we called Soft Feet?" Tara asked.

"Tara, you didn't know who I was?" Joseph asked.

"No!" Tara said.

"Tara, I've liked you since we were kids. I knew who you were when we were in court." Joseph said.

"Hello, again Tara." Mike said.

"Who the fuck is you?" Joseph looked at Tara waiting on her to answer his question.

"Hi, my name is Mike." He introduced himself.

"I don't give a fuck who you are. Step your Payless Shoe wearing ass off my wife!" Joseph said aggressively.

"I didn't know. I'm sorry." Mike said and walked away.

"How in the hell he know your name?" Joseph asked Tara.

"When we were getting on the plane, they gave the ticket back to me, and the stewardess said, Tara, have a nice time." Tara said to Joseph.

"Tara don't forget what I told you about these niggas." Joseph said.

"How long is the plane ride gonna take?" Tara asked.

"About two and an half hours, why you have something planned?" Joseph said.

"Joseph, don't start." Tara rolled her eyes at Joseph.

"Peggy, Joseph is going to hurt somebody about Tara." Red said as he was eavesdropping on their conversation.

Red looked over at Karen and his brother all snuggled up in their seats. Red whispered to Peggy, "Damn and JaDarrell fell head over hills for Karen."

"She fell for him, too." Peggy said as she closed her eyes and enjoyed her flight.

Chapter 11

As the Pilot told the passengers they were about to land and asked everyone to buckle their seat belts, Peggy and her entire entourage woke up from their brief nap.

"That was a nice quick ride. Now we need to go to baggage claim and get our luggage. We need to be thinking about what hotel we are going to lay our heads while we are in the Big Apple." Peggy said to her family.

"We're going to stay at the Hilton. We got to get rooms for Paul, Pam, Joe and Kezia. They should be here in an hour." Tara said to her sister.

"Tara, call and leave a message on Pam and Kezia's phones to let them know what hotel we are at and how to get here okay?" Peggy said to her sister.

"Girl this place is so busy. Everyone is moving so fast." Tara said.

"Red, did you get Karen her room by herself?" Peggy asked.

"I will get it." Red said.

"I don't need you to worry about Karen." JaDarrell interjected.

"Well, excuse me!" Peggy said and snaked her neck.

"I need two rooms." Karen said.

"No, we need one room." JaDarrell said.

"What, Karen you need your room to yourself." Peggy asked trying to figure out what had just happened. They were all lovey dovey on the flight.

"Tara and Peggy, I'm twenty-five years old, I can think for myself. One please!" Karen said.

"Little sister told both big sisters something!" JaDarrell chimed in supporting his boo.

"Here are the keys for Pam and Kezia. This is what you call life after the ghetto Fo' sho! Just being able to hop on plane and go anywhere in the United States you wanna go. We are all meeting up when Paul gets here." Peggy said.

Karen asked, "JaDarrell, what are you getting ready to do, take a shower?

"Wash my ass." JaDarrell laughed. He knew that Karen wanted her own room because she didn't want to be giving it up so soon. He knew he had to convince her that the time didn't matter.

While JaDarrell gets in the shower, Karen went into the bedroom and removed her clothes and went into the bathroom and opened the shower door. Standing there with nothing on JaDarrell got hard.

"Karen asked softly, "Can I join you?"

Darrell helped her into the shower and they started kissing. He started sucking her breast, making her pussy wet. Then JaDarrell asked Karen, "Karen, can I make love to you?"

"JaDarrell wait, I never had sex before."

He picked her and took her to the bedroom and laid her on the bed and started kissing her all over her neck and back up to her mouth.

"Karen are you sure about this?" he asked.

She nodded and agreement and he went a step further. When JaDarrell was putting the head of his penis in Karen, she was so tight and Karen hollered so loud that he stopped. He stopped and grabbed the some lubricant to rub on his manhood.

Karen told him how she wanted to remember this night. So, JaDarrell started back and the pain was so bad that Karen kept on hollering and scratching up JaDarrell's back. JaDarrell was being easy with her. JaDarrell had a large penis. After fifteen minutes, Karen started moving with him. JaDarrell put about half in because he didn't want to hurt her too much. It was feeling so good that Karen told him to put it all in, so he put all twelve inches in her.

Karen told JaDarrell to kiss her. Their mouths met and Darrell flipped over on his back and told Karen to ride him. Darrell started sucking on her breast as she eased down on is large penis taking as much as she could. After twenty minutes of riding his dick, it started feeling good to Karen. She was still hollering and talking to him, telling him how he felt so good inside of her.

"JaDarrell, I love this!" Karen said as her juices began running all over JaDarrell's dick. JaDarrell started pushing more dick up in her. Then Karen felt the biggest nut. She started hollering, "JaDarrell, I'm coming!" she was shaking and hollering. And still saying she was coming as JaDarrell told her to ride it on out. Little did JaDarrell know that Karen fell in love that day? JaDarrell flipped her on her back and climbed on top of her and made love to her so good that about an hour until they both bust again! But little did they know that they made a baby that day.

JaDarrell got up and ran them some bath water. "Karen, are you alright?" he asked.

"Yes, JaDarrell, I'm fine as hell! But I'm sore as hell." Karen said.

"So, Karen, do this means that you're my lady now?" he asked.

"JaDarrell, I became your lady when I first saw you." Karen said.

"I got the nice one out of the family." JaDarrell said.

"No baby, Red got the nice one." Karen kissed him on his forehead and smiled.

"What? Peggy will take a nigger's head off!" JaDarrell trying to hold his composure.

"Sweetheart, listen to what I say. Peggy is the nice one out of my daddy's kids!" Karen said.

"So where do you fall in the group of nineteen?" JaDarrell asked.

"JaDarrell, I really can't tell you. I'm like number sixteen. How many kids does your parents have?" Karen asked.

"That's easy. It's only five of us. Red, me, Janet, Keisha and Devontae!"

"Where's your mother?"

"In Texas."

"So, what do you do in Texas?" JaDarrell asked.

"I teach fourth grade and I dibble and dabble in Real Estate."

"Peggy, didn't tell me that."

"Because they do not know! I've been doing it for about two years now."

Karen cell phone began to ring. She saw it was her sister. She picked it up to answer, "Hey Kezia!"

"They want us all to meet in the lobby in one hour." Kezia said.

"JaDarrell, I'm walking funny and I'm sore." Karen said.

"Baby, you're walking the same." JaDarrell said.

"You sure?" Karen asked.

"Yes, I'm sure. Karen, are you ready?" JaDarrell asked.

"How do I look?"

"Karen, put on the rest of your outfit!"

"This is the whole outfit."

"I'm going to jail! Let's go."

They left out of their hotel room and went to wait in the lobby like Kezia said.

"Where is everybody at, Karen?" Kezia asked.

"Paul, Kezia oh I miss y'all. How have you been?" Karen hugged her siblings.

"Fine." They both said in unison.

"You know when J.J.'s kids to get together, we haven't seen each other in about three years." Karen said.

"Kezia, baby come her for a minute." Joe said.

"Joe, Red is married to Peggy. JaDarrell is with Karen." Paul said.

"What, little sister with JaDarrell now?" Kezia asked.

"Yes, is that a problem?" JaDarrell asked.

"No." Kezia said as she turn to her sister introducing herself to Joe.

"Hello, I'm Karen, Kezia's sister."

"Hi, I'm Joe, Kezia's husband." Joe said as he hugged Kezia.

"Welcome to the family." Karen said and turned to a familiar face, "Hey Pam!"

"Hi Karen!" Pam said in return.

"Can we have a table for ten?" Peggy said to the hostess.

"Right this way." The hostess led them to their table.

"Hey, Joe!" Pam said.

"How you doing Red and JaDarrell?" Joe said.

"Cool man." Red replied.

"Nigga I didn't know that you was married to Peggy! Hell didn't know that you were a couple." Joe said.

"Eight years, and now we are a family." Red replied.

"Red man, Kezia is the best thing that ever happened to me." Joe said.

"Now you know how I feel about, Peggy. JaDarrell tried to get with Karen hard." Red said.

"Nigger please, I'm here from the way she stepped to me." JaDarrell said. They all started laughing.

"And now Tara is my sister-in-law. Shit the one that shot me and now we are family. She doesn't take any shit." Red said.

"Kezia don't play, we was at the spot and JoAnne, the girl I used to fuck with, the girl kept pulling on me, all up in my face. I told the girl to move and she kept on. Kezia took a beer bottle and slapped her in the face with it, her friends stood up and Pam pulled a gun on those bitches so fast. Man, I don't know about you and JaDarrell but I'm here to stay!" Joe said.

"Joe man, I'm here to stay Fo' Sho." JaDarrell said.

"I know both of you heard how Baby D was putting down the cross on me with that nigga Pete. But I'm gonna kill both of those bitch ass niggas." Joe said.

"We heard but we family now." Red said.

"Thanks man. And it hurts me when Baby D crossed me like that. He started being funny when me and Kezia got married." Joe said.

"Joseph, where have you been?" Tara asked.

"I'll tell everybody later when Tara is not around. We better get to the club before them sisters start clicking." Peggy said.

"Ha, my sisters don't play!" Kezia said.

"We know. And guess what Paul?" Tara said.

"What?" Paul asked.

"That goes for Pam." Tara said.

"Yeah. Now you niggas tell me that after she slapped the shit out of me!" Paul said.

"Here's comes Peggy, let's go!" Pam said.

"I was coming to tell you the music is cool! In New York, not our kind of music." Kezia said.

"Oh shit, what they know about Lil Wayne? Now they playing 50 cent. What they know about the Cupid Slide? Shit we taking over the floor!" Tara said.

"One thing about St. Louis people, we can dress and dance our ass off!" Peggy said.

"Where are our ladies?" Joseph asked.

"Still on the dance floor!" Paul said.

"Look at these sons of bitches looking at our wives! JaDarrell man, do you see what I see?" Red asked.

"What, how the fuck does Karen move her hips like that?" JaDarrell asked.

"Shit Karen, all of them moving their hips and butts like that!" Joseph said, "Man, I'm going to catch a case!"

"Not the lawyer going to catch a case!" Paul laughed extremely hard. He stopped laughing as he saw a guy walk over to Pam. He looked very serious when he said, "Look at that nigga going to dance with Pam, fuck this shit, time to go!"

Joseph could no longer watch the strip tease the girls were partaking in while on the dance floor. He walked over to his girl. He grabbed her arm and said, "Tara, let's go."

The girls watched as Tara was being escorted from the dance floor. When Peggy looked over and notice that the rest of the guys were not pleased by what they were watching on the dance floor, she informed the girls. The agreed that they would all leave and head back to their hotel rooms. Everyone wasn't ready to end the night. They agreed to all meet in one room. They would decide whose room when they got upstairs.

Chapter 12

"Is everybody here?" Peggy asked.

"Not Joseph!" Kezia said.

"I'm here." Joseph said as he entered when Kezia said his name.

"Alright, let's get started!" Peggy said.

"What about?" Paul asked.

"We are all family. Now some are just girlfriends and boyfriends, but we are all family. So what are we going to do about St. Louis?" Peggy said.

"Kezia and I are not going back. When I go back it will be for Baby D and Pete, I'm going to kill those punk ass niggas!" Joe said.

"Well, me and Peggy not going back." Red said.

"Well, me and Karen not back to St. Louis either." JaDarrell said.

"Everybody knows damn well me and Pam are not going." Paul said.

"Well, my job is in St. Louis but I don't feel right with Tara in St. Louis and I'm not getting ready to let another man push up on my lady so I left my job as of this morning." Joseph said.

Joseph was talking to Red about his future plans as Joe entered the room. Joe and Red really didn't have much of a conversation prior to their girls being partners. They knew mutual people and some of the company they kept didn't get along with one another. They quickly set their differences aside.

"Well, Joe, you know we are family now and when you go for Baby D, we got your back!" Red said.

"Thanks bro-in-law but when I go, I'm going for both!" Joe said looking at Joseph wondering if he really wanted to talk about this in front of the lawyer in the room.

"Joe, you know Pete is dead?" Red shared the news he had recently heard.

"What?" Joe was shocked because he had not heard about his death.

"Yeah. We saw it on the news when were at the airport." Red said.

"Well everybody, do not forget that Baby D stills calls me." Pam said as she entered the room hearing part of the conversation.

"What you mean he still call you? Have you been talking to him?" Paul inquired.

"No, Paul. He keeps leaving messages on my voicemail." Pam reassured him.

"Let's see where his head is at, call him, Pam." Joe said.

Pam picked up her cellphone to call Baby D, "Wait everybody, and be real quiet."

"Pam, put it on speaker." Red instructed.

The phone began to ring. Everyone sat quietly waiting on Baby D to answer. As soon as they heard his voice everyone sat back to take it all in.

"Yeah, Baby D, what's up?" Pam said.

"Who is this?" Baby D asked.

"Pam."

"Where are you?"

"In New York."

"So, you just left without telling me shit! I came home to cook motherfucking dinner and I called you and your ass say you at the mall. Now you call me two weeks later and tell me your ass is in New York, what the fuck is going on?" Baby D said with anger in his voice.

"I was calling you to tell you that I'll be home next week." Pam said as she shrugged her shoulders.

"And where the fuck is Kezia?" Baby D asked.

"What you mean where is Kezia? That last time I talked to her, she said that she was going with Joe somewhere. And she has not answered her phone ever since then." Pam said.

"Joe hasn't called me. I just came from a wake." Baby D said.

"Who died?" Pam asked, really not caring.

"This dude named Pete got killed." Baby D said as he rubbed his head.

"That's why I don't like it down there! I got to find out where Kezia is." Pam said.

"If you talk to her before I do, tell Joe to holler at me. And you better get your ass here by Saturday, you hear with the fuck I said?" Baby D instructed.

"Yeah, Baby D! I'll be there." Pam lied.

"And don't let me call your damn phone and you don't answer, Pam!" Baby D said.

"Yeah." Pam agreed.

"I have to come up there next Monday and handle some business, have yo ass packed and ready to go that night alright?" Baby D raised his voice and spoke firmly.

"Baby D, why are you hollering at me?" Pam asked.

"Pam, my lady up and left, somebody stole my 6.5 million dollars from out of my house and blew it up, Joe haven't called or answered his phone. I'm starting all over again so why the fuck you think I'm hollering? I am coming to New York and I'll see you Monday night." Baby D said his peace and hung up the phone.

"Pam, it's a setup! The nigga don't do business up there. The Connect is L.A. and goes by the name of Butter because he is so light-skinned." Joe said.

"Why the fuck would he be trying to set me up? Shit ain't that serious." Pam said.

"I can't call it with Baby D right now. We just have to sit back and watch this shit play out. I just know shit get fucked up more every day." Joe said.

Every one said their good nights and their see you tomorrows. Once that took place everyone departed and head to their respected destination.

Joseph and Tara were sitting in their hotel room. They were sitting quietly as Joseph thumbed to the channels. He laid the remote down and went to the bathroom. He flushed the toilet opened the door and stuck his head out the door and asked Tara, "Do you want to go shopping in the morning?" he began to wash his hands as he waited on her response.

"That's fine." Tara just agreed.

"Let's get in the shower so we can get in the bed." Joseph said.

"Where's my house coat?" Tara asked.

"Hanging up. Let's get in the bed, can we make love?" Joseph said in one breath.

"Yeah." Tara said.

Joseph was all over Tara before she could even answer his question.

"Oh shit, oh baby it hurts! Stop!" Tara moaned.

"All that hollering, come on and shake those hips like you was doing on the dance floor." Joseph said.

"Joseph, it hurts!" Tara complained.

"Stop crying Tara. Alright, I'll stop. You only dance like that at home." Joseph gathered himself and rose from the bed, "Make sure to get you an outfit out for the morning, we are getting married!" Joseph said.

"No, we are not!" Tara disagreed.

"Yea, we are. Tara, I have been in love with you since high school and you think I'm going to let you leave me. Stop crying baby. Pass me the phone. Hey Red, call everyone and tell them to be ready by 10:30, me and Tara are getting married!" Joseph said.

"What! Cool man. Wait, Peggy here." Red said.

"Joseph, what's going on?" Peggy said.

"Tara and I are getting married in the morning!" Joseph said to Peggy.

Peggy said a few more words with Joseph and hung up the phone. She called Paul be he didn't answer so she called her sister Karen. Karen answered immediately.

"Hello, Karen?" Peggy said as soon as she heard Karen's voice.

"Yeah." Karen answered.

"Everybody has to be ready in the morning!" Peggy said with excitement in her voice.

Karen found out why Peggy was so excited. She let her sister know that they would be ready. Peggy told her they will talk in the morning because she had other calls to make.

Karen wasn't off the phone good before JaDarrell was all over her. "Wait JaDarrell, is it going to hurt again?" she asked as he began to kiss her on her inner thighs.

"I don't know. If it does, tell me and I'll stop. Open your legs a little more." JaDarrell said.

"JaDarrell baby, oh JaDarrell, oh baby that shit still hurts." Karen moaned.

JaDarrell started kissing and sucking her going all the way down and kissing her inner thigh and sucking her pussy. Karen started moving her hips and throwing her pussy back in his face and came three times. JaDarrell climbed back on her and rode her like she was the only woman in the world that mattered and falling in love with her more and more every minute. Forty-five minutes later JaDarrell starts hollering, "I'm coming, oh Karen, I'm coming, oh shit!"

"Sweetheart, you ok?"

"Yeah, let's take a shower!"

"Oh shit JaDarrell, I'm so sore."

"I'm sorry baby. Do that mean we can't have sex tomorrow?"

"No, it don't JaDarrell."

Chapter 13

"Damn, Tara looks so pretty. And Paul was here to give her away. Joseph looks so happy and Tara too! But she know that she can't run over him. Throw the rice everybody." Peggy said excited as can be.

After the wedding everyone was packed up and ready to head to their destination. A planned two week trip turned into a four week stay. Tara and Joseph flew to Las Vegas to their new house. Red and Peggy flew to Florida. JaDarrell and Karen flew to Texas. Kezia and Joe flew to their new house that Joe had never told anyone about in Phoenix. And Paul and Pam flew back south until Karen found them a house in Phoenix. They all agreed to meet back up with each other in two weeks.

Two weeks later Karen was very sick and JaDarrell took her to the doctor's office and found out that he was going to be a daddy. Karen let JaDarrell know she was six weeks pregnant. He was so happy he called everybody to tell them he was going to be daddy.

"Damn little brother, I'm happy for you! I'll be glad when Peggy gets pregnant." Red said.

"Where is my sister-in-law?" JaDarrell asked.

"On the beach. JaDarrell, I was going to call you and talk to you." Red said.

"About what?" JaDarrell asked.

"Man, we got too got to St. Louis." Red said.

"For what?" JaDarrell asked.

"Man, Peggy got a phone call about twenty minutes ago and their daddy is sick, very sick. I got to tell her when she gets here. The doctor called her cell phone." Red said.

"Damn Red, let me go and tell Karen. We gonna have to start packing. Did you tell Tara and Kezia?" JaDarrell asked.

"Not yet. I'm getting ready to call Joe and Joseph now. I need you to call Pam and tell her so she can tell Paul." Red said.

"Alright, Red. I'll let you go so you can make your phone calls." JaDarrell said.

"Here comes Peggy now. Hey JaDarrell, you have Pam's number?" Red said.

"Yeah." JaDarrell said.

"Cool. Call Pam for me." Red said.

Peggy came in with a smile on face, "Red baby let's go out to dinner tonight."

"Peggy, baby sit down." Red instructed.

"Baby, what's wrong?" Peggy asked.

"Peggy, your daddy is real sick, we have to go to St. Louis." Red said.

"What the fuck you mean he is sick!" Peggy shouted.

"The doctor called your cell phone. They need you to get there."

"No! Red, don't tell me this shit!" Peggy said.

"I'm sorry baby. Go ahead baby, you can cry." Red said as he embraced her.

"What happened?" Peggy said with tears in her eyes.

"I don't know. The doctor said he will talk to you when you get there." Red had to adjust to grab his phone from off the bed, "Wait baby let me get the phone. Yeah. What's up Joseph? I know man Peggy is going crazy too! We gonna catch a flight out tonight about 6:45. He's in Barnes Hospital."

"Red, man me and Tara are leaving in about one hour so we will see you there, alright?" Joseph said.

"Cool. This Joe calling my cell phone right now." Red clicked over, "Hey what's up?"

"You got it Red. Man how is Peggy doing?" Joe asked.

"She's not." Red said.

"Kezia is the same way and Tara, too. Well we have a plane going to St. Louis non-stop leaving in about two hours so we will be there. What hospital is he in?" Joe asked.

"Barnes." Red said.

"Alright." Joe said.

"Hey Joe, I got us some rooms at the Marriot West on Maryville center Drive." Red said.

"That's cool. I will see you later." Joe said.

"Peggy baby you ready, our plane leaves in forty-five minutes." Red said.

"Yeah, let's go!" Peggy said.

Two and a half hours later Peggy and Red was at the hospital. Peggy didn't pay attention to nothing what was going on. All she was worried about was her dad.

"Yes, we are here to see Jarrell Johnson, I'm his daughter Peggy."

"Peggy baby, here is Joseph and JaDarrell." Red said.

"Peggy, third floor. Let's go." Tara said.

"Red, what's the doctor's name?" Peggy asked.

"Dr. Black." Red said.

"Robin." Peggy called out.

"Hey Peggy, how are you doing?" Robin asked.

"Fine sis, have anybody talked to the doctor?" Peggy said.

"Jamel and Travon did." Robin said.

"Where are they?" Peggy asked.

"In the room with Tara, Karen and Kezia. Robert and J. J. Jr. went to pick up Paul from the airport." Robin said.

"Alright, let me go and see my daddy." Peggy said.

"Hey sis, you doing alright?" Jamel asked.

"Fine I guess. Jamel, how is he doing?" Peggy asked.

"Not good." Jamel said.

Red and Joseph came and to get Peggy and Tara. Joe eventually came in to get Kezia. They were trying their best to comfort the girls. It was hard when no one had any answers to what was going on with their dad. They didn't know how the next chapter in J.J.'s life was about to turn out.

"What the fuck happened?" Peggy asked with frustration in her voice.

"Wait till Paul and TeTe and Yane get here and we all can talk." Robin said.

"Where the fuck are they?" Peggy asked.

"Here they all come now, everybody let's go to the room over there. So, Travon can you tell us what is going on? Karen come over here." Robin said.

"Where the fuck is Sherry?" Peggy said.

"Fuck her?" Tara said.

"Close the door." Robin said.

"Travon, what's going on?" Peggy asked.

"Somebody shot daddy three times." Travon said.

"What? Where the fuck was he?" Peggy asked.

"Pop was at the junkyard at his desk, the police don't have any leads is all I know." Travon said.

"Jamel, what about the tape?" Peggy turned to her other brother that was next to Travon.

"What tape?" Travon asked.

"I put cameras all around the junkyard and in his office." Peggy said.

"Peggy, Are you sure because the police didn't say anything about any tape?" Jamel asked.

"They said all the money was gone." Travon said.

"Wait, Peggy put cameras up?" Karen asked.

"Yeah." Robin said.

"What's up, Karen?" Travon asked.

"Fuck this shit! Jamel, Paul and Glenn. Go to the junkyard and get those tapes and bring them to the hotel." Peggy said.

"Peggy, how many cameras are up there?" Travon asked.

"It's seven." Peggy answered.

"Then there got to be at least seven tapes. Peggy tell them how to get the tapes and where to look for them." Karen said.

"Robert, you watch, their back. You get those motherfucking tapes now!" Peggy said to her other brother.

"We are at the Marriot West Hotel. Here come Kelly and Sherry. Don't say shit to anybody!" Karen said.

"Hey, sis, how is he?" Sherry asked.

"Not good at all." Peggy said.

"Kelly and Sherry, we are getting ready to go to the hotel, you two stay here at the hospital with daddy. Kelly call me if anything happens." Peggy said.

"Okay, sis." Sherry said.

"Give me a hug. Love you." Peggy said.

"I love you, too." Sherry said.

"Alright, let's go." Peggy said.

"Red and JaDarrell, make sure we have something to play those tapes on. Joe and Joseph, get the room together so we can go over the tapes." Tara said.

"The rooms have DVD and VCR players in them." Red said.

"Alright. Whose phone playing 50 cent song?" Tara asked.

The boys went to retrieve the tapes from the junkyard. Travon had to call Peggy and find out what hotel they were at. Peggy was growing impatient as she waited on her brothers to get there with the tapes. As soon as they arrived they were not in the hotel room good before Peggy had pressed play. Peggy was so pissed when she saw Baby D and Eric, Ann's little brother on the tape. She vowed that Baby D was going to die one way or another. She held back tears as she thought on how she was going to bring him down.

Chapter 14

Jarell Johnson looked around his hospital room the only person he saw was Travon. He didn't make a difference with in his children, he just knew who was more responsible and loyal to his well-being. He needed to know where his Jr. was When J.J. Jr. made his presence, he let him know that they needed to get Peggy up there. Travon called Peggy and let her know that she needed to get up to the hospital. Peggy didn't ask why, she left the hotel and was there in fifteen minutes. He informed his children that he had been betrayed by his own blood. From the look in Peggy's eyes her blood was boiling. She couldn't even ask questions. Her dad always told her that blood didn't make you family. Listening to her dad made her realize what he meant over the years.

She had a strong feeling who was behind this. She needed to hear it from her dad. When he said that two of his daughters set him up, Peggy was all ears. She wanted him to release the names. She needed to know who she had to kill. The only problem is that one of her brother or sisters wouldn't agree.

Peggy knew the disagreement would come up with her siblings. J.J. had nineteen kids. All of his children were close and they knew each other. The closeness was established according to what siblings had the same mother.

"Daddy, I can't take it any longer. You need to tell me who is behind this?" Peggy said.

He took a deep breath, "Paula and Sherry."

Tears began to fall and Peggy shouted, "What the hell did you just say?"

"Stay away from them." J.J. said.

"I'll kill those bitches!" Peggy screamed.

"Wait Peggy, we got to come up with a plan." Travon said.

"Fuck that, I plan on killing those whores, that's my plan." Peggy said.

"Wait Peggy we have to think, calm down." Travon said.

Peggy reached down in her purse. She was digging for so long, she forgot she was reaching in her purse to make a phone call. As soon as she retrieved her phone she called Red.

"Red, I need you to get JaDarrell. Then get Joseph and Joe on the phone one by one and tell them to go get our shit out of the hotel. Don't tell anyone what's going on." Peggy said.

"Peggy, what's wrong?" Red asked because Peggy had called him to give him instructions with an explanation.

"Don't call my name, baby." Peggy said.

"Peggy, I'm down the hall talking to you." Red said while he was walking in the hospital heading towards Peggy.

"Call JaDarrell and I will call Joseph. Paul will you let Joe know what's going on. You go and talk to Joe and checkout of the hotel and fund us somewhere for us to stay alright. And don't say shit!" Peggy said to Red. That just made him turn around and go do what his wife asked of him.

"Pop, are you sure about this?" Travon asked.

"Yeah, son."

"Daddy, here comes Yane and TeTe." Peggy said.

"Well, Jarrell Johnson, how do you feel?" Yane asked.

"I'm in pain but I'll be okay." J.J. said.

"Yane and TeTe stay here, we got get us a hotel room." Travon said.

"No, Tete and Yane go with Peggy and don't tell anyone where you are staying." J.J. said.

"Peggy, what's going on?" TeTe asked.

"We will talk later and I will fill you in TeTe. Hey Jamel, tell everybody to come on in." Peggy said.

"Hey daddy, how you feel?" Yane asked.

"Fucked up!" J.J. said.

"Damn, Tara, why is it taking so long for everybody to come in, I thought we were going to talk about what has happened?" Sherry said.

"When we talk, the whole family will be there to talk." Peggy said.

"Peggy, did Red go?" Sherry asked.

"I told him to give some time with daddy. Why Sherry? What's wrong?" Peggy asked.

"Nothing. I thought he went to get some food. Pam and Joe went to eat. Peggy, your phone is ringing." Sherry said.

"Hello." Peggy said and she stop to listen to what Red had to tell her about what had just taken place. He along with the others, had all checked out of the hotel. Joseph contacted one of his lawyer friends. His friend just so had one of his rental properties available. He only used it for family's that were vacationing anyway and they were in luck. It was vacant at the current moment. Joseph believed it had twelve bedrooms. He was wasn't for sure but he said they would make it work. Before Red ended his call, he let her know to not say a word to anyone of what was going on.

JaDarrell was sitting in the waiting room of the hospital watching how Karen was sitting in the chair. He asked her was she okay and she lied and said yes. She was really getting restless and the chair was very uncomfortable for her. JaDarrell didn't believe her when she responded.

JaDarrell turned to Kezia, "You know Karen really needs to go lay down for a while, you know she's pregnant?"

"Okay, we leave at two at a time first it will be JaDarrell and Karen, then Joe and I and then Robert, Jamel and Travon and then Yane and Tete and Pam and Paul then Joseph and Tara." Kezia felt that the shifts would work and someone would at least be with her dad at all times.

Sherry had said she wasn't going anywhere. She just needed something to eat because she was hungry. Once she had put something on her stomach she would be cool. Tara let her know that she would walk with her to get something to eat because she wanted a cup of coffee.

"Karen, JaDarrell, Kezia, and Joe wants you. Jamel, Robert, Travon, and J.J., go with them, Hurry before Sherry come back." Peggy took a deep breath, "Pam, when Sherry comes back, you, Tee and Yane leave to get something to eat and Paul, you know what to do right?"

"Peggy, what's going on?" Peggy turned to see if Sherry was with Tara. Tara let her know that Sherry told her she would bring her cup of coffee back up with her. She let Peggy know she didn't have a good feeling and she needed to go check on there with her dad. She walked towards the hospital room that wasn't nothing but three rooms away from the family waiting room.

Peggy walked with Tara. When they entered the room their dad was mumbling about his shooters. Peggy walked over to his bedside, "Tara, we'll talk later. Shut up J.J., you're crazy and just half sleep."

"Bullshit! You can think I'm sleep." J.J. said to his daughter.

J.J. cell phone began to ring. He told Peggy to answer his phone. The call came with no name so she gave the phone to Tara.

Tara looked at Peggy as though she was crazy but she answered anyway, "Hello."

"This is Kevin. May I ask who am I speaking with?"

"Hey there big brother. This is Tara."

"How's Pop doing?"

"He comes and goes."

"Where are you at baby sis?" Kevin asked.

"I'm right here in his room with him." Tara said.

"I see we are getting ready to leave soon. I'm going to stay and keep an eye on pop. J. J. and Glenn knows how to reach out and touch me." Peggy said.

"But Peggy, Travon and Jamel called a family meeting." Tara said to Peggy. She continued to with her brother Kevin, "Why aren't you up here?"

"I'm keeping a low profile, J. J. will let me know. Put Peggy on the phone." Kevin said. "Peggy, how you doing?"

"I'm cool." Peggy told her brother.

"Peggy, check this out, keep your eyes on Yane and TeTe." Kevin informed her.

"Why?" Peggy asked.

"Because they ass will go off shooting up some shit." Kevin said.

"Kevin, we need to talk." Peggy said.

"We will but not right now." Kevin shot back.

"I will be here all night." Peggy said feeling like she needed to stay right beside her dad. "Hey Kevin, Sherry is up here and I don't think you need to let her see you."

"Why?" Kevin asked.

"Just don't alright?" Peggy said.

"I love you, sis." Kevin said.

"I love you, too." Peggy said.

Peggy walked back to the waiting area to see what was going on with her family. "Pam, here comes Sherry so everybody go ahead and leave." Peggy said.

"Sherry, this my coffee?" Tara said as she reached for the cup.

"Yeah." Sherry said.

"TeTe were you and Yane going to eat? Wait me and Paul going too." Pam said.

"Tara, here come Joseph and Red, too." Peggy said.

"Tara, baby have you eating anything?" Joseph asked.

"Peggy and Tara, I will stay here with daddy tonight and everybody just come back in the morning because J. J. is in the chair sleep." Sherry said.

"Sherry, are you sure?" Peggy asked.

"Yeah." Sherry said.

"Alright! J.J. wakes all the way up, gives us a call. Sherry, me and Peggy will be back here about nine in the morning." Tara said.

"Cool." Sherry said.

Peggy walked back in the room with her dad. She whispered in his ear, "J. J. call Kevin and tell him we are leaving and Sherry is still here."

"He knows, he's looking at us." J.J. said.

"Where the fuck is Kevin?" Peggy looked around with confused look.

"Peggy, I got this. You all go ahead and get some rest."

They all got ready to leave the hospital and Tara turns to Peggy and says, "Girl, yo daddy has too many damn kids."

They all were quiet and resting while they were heading to the place that they were going to rest up.

"Damn Joseph, where did you get this house from? This house is huge!" Tara said.

Peggy called everyone to the living room in the place they were staying. She waited on everyone to get comfortable before she started talking. When she seen everyone was cool she began to speak.

"Well let's get this started. Go ahead Travon and Robert. Before they get started, Yane, TeTe and Glenn stay cool." Peggy said.

"What the fuck you mean stay cool!" Yane yelled.

"Just listen Yane, alright?" Peggy said.

"Cool." Yane agreed.

"The people that shot daddy was looking for Kezia and Joe." Travon said.

"You mean these punk as nigga was looking for me and my wife! I'm killing they bitch ass and their families!" Joe screamed.

"Wait Joe, there's more." Peggy said.

"But Travon, how did they know I was Jarrell's daughter?" Kezia asked.

"Sherry and Paula told them, they was there, waiting outside in the car." Travon said.

"Fuck that, I'm killing those snake ass bitches." TeTe jumped up.

"Calm down TeTe, comeback here Yane." Peggy went after her brother.

"Fuck that Peggy is this true?" Yane asked.

"Yeah, that's what daddy told us when he had woke up." Peggy said.

"We left that bitch there to keep him!" Karen and Tara said in unison.

"Don't be crazy Tara and Karen, Kevin is there keeping a low profile, watching Sherry." Peggy said.

"Where the fuck is Paula staying?" Tara said.

"We don't know, I think that bitch is smoking that shit!" Peggy said.

"Let's come up with a plan, Karen." Tara turned to her younger sister.

"I got a plan, I'm going to Kill Sherry, Paula, Baby D and his family." Joe said.

"JaDarrell, talk to Karen. Joe please talk to Kezia and Joseph, Tara is leaving go get her! Pam where is Paul?" Peggy was getting antsy trying to keep everyone cool

"He's on the phone. Glenn, J.J., Kevin and Paul are all on the phone talking." Karen said.

Peggy and her brothers discussed somethings. JaDarrell left out to go to Imo's to pick up some pizza. Peggy let them know she was about to take a shower so she could relax. Everyone else dozed off to get some rest until JaDarrell had made it back with the food. Everything was calm until Kezia just all of a sudden snapped.

LIFE AFTER THE GHETTO

"Red, where the hell is Peggy?" Joe asked because he didn't know what to do at this point.

"She's still in the shower." Red said.

"Tell her to get her ass down here and calm her sis the fuck down! I can't handle her right now!" Joe said.

No one had to go get Peggy. She heard all the commotion and headed back to the living room where her family was.

"Hey calm your assess down, what the fuck is going on in here?" Peggy wasn't understanding what was going on.

"Your sister trying to get the fuck out of the house!" Joe yelled.

"Everybody sit down." Peggy said calmly making sure she didn't add fuel to the fire.

"Fuck that Glenn, that bitch got to die!" Kezia said to her brother.

"Shut up and sit down now!" Peggy said.

Way across town Baby D was during his normal thing. He was feeling like he had got his lick back. He had been betrayed. His empire had been destroyed and he was doing everything he could to rebuild.

"Baby D man, where are you going nigga?" his homeboy wanted to make sure he was watching his back. Things were hot for them at the moment.

"Up on Schulte, I got a sell for two keys." Baby D said.

"Man if they over there gambling call me."

"Nigga, that's all they do. Shit, them Schulte boys are playing poker." Baby D said.

Baby d was on the Schulte about to get rid of his work, "Hey Rick where's Bobby?"

"Bobby and Eric went on Era to check on the traps. Then they are going up on Mimika to shoot some dice with the Emma boys. That nigga Quick is going to keep their ass in the poor house with that gambling shit." Rick said.

"Bobby doesn't like Quick." Baby D said.

"That's because he's fucking Quick's baby momma! But those twins will fuck his ass up!" Rick said.

"Shit his old dude will, too." Baby D said.

"Baby D, what are we going to do about those two bitches?" Rick asked.

"We are going to use them for a little while and then kill those whores." Baby D said.

"Man, that bitch Sherry can suck the shit out of some dick! That bitch will have you swinging from left to right." Rick said.

"Man you crazy than a motherfucker!" Baby D laughed.

"Baby D, man we got to get all the players on Mimika, Schulte, Era, Emma and Floy and have our own award show for the bitches that suck the best dick man. The hoes will be coming from everywhere trying to win the damn prize." Rick laughed.

"Man, carry your sick ass to bed!" Baby D said as he turned to leave.

"Man, fuck you Bye!" Rick said.

Meanwhile Baby D was thinking he had killed J.J. and he was laying in the hospital bed wide awoke and recovering. His sons were plotting his revenge.

"Glenn, what's up, do you Kevin and J.J. have a plan?"

"Yes, we do! Paula lives on Riverview. We have TeTe and Yane watching her ass now. The bitch will fuck up and when she does, we got her!"

"Why the hell would you send TeTe, he's too hot headed!" Jamel said, "Yane on the phone now. I love all my brothers but my sisters will handle this shit."

"Karen, baby sis what are you talking about? Paula just went to the Gasmart by her house Yane said. So, I told TeTe when that bitch gets back home, kill her ass. And whoever has something to say, step up now!" Peggy said.

"Don't even give that bitch time to explain shit. Dead that hoe!" Karen said.

JaDarrell was shocked when he heard Karen speak. He turned to Peggy, "Man, I thought she was the nice one."

"I told everybody Peggy is the nice sister! And don't get Tara going."

Tara had heard enough. She couldn't believe that her sister were behind her dad getting shot. When she heard that Paula had left Memphis and found her a spot near Mimika it kind of pissed her off. As much as her dad tried to instill in them loyalty amongst all their siblings, she couldn't believe that the family had been infiltrated by their own blood. Seeds of J.J. tried to destroy him. She knew in her heart that something needed to be done. Tara felt that there was no time for a plan. No one needed to be around to retaliate. She was headed to go see Paula and it wasn't going to end nicely.

"Who is it?" Paula went to answer the knock on the door.

"It's me, sis." Tara said as calmly as possible.

Paula wanted to know how Tara knew where to find her. She didn't ask because she didn't want to appear suspicious. Tara didn't care about trying to feel around or figure her out. She came there for one reason only. Before Paula could speak she saw the barrel of Tara's gun. With a blink of an eye Paula hit the floor. She was dead and Tara knew it. Tara mission had been accomplished. She left out the house as quiet as she came. She headed to her next victim. Sherry was no longer going to sit by her father side as though she was not responsible for him laying up in that hospital bed.

Tara was taking her drive to the hospital. She was thinking how she was going to get Sherry. As soon as she pulled up to the hospital she saw this lady leave her car for valet. She gave her car to the valet driver and hopped in the car she saw that no one was paying attention to. She called Sherry and told her to come to the side where the cars were being valeted. Sherry was there like Johnny on the spot. She saw Tara and walked to get in the car. Tara pulled around the corner. Sherry didn't know what hit her. Tara got out the car and put the gun in her purse. She walked up to the valet driver, waited for her car and when her car arrived she was out. She had head back to the house they were staying in. As soon as she walked in the door Joseph called for her.

"Tara, baby can I talk to you!" Joseph said firmly.

"Sure, Joseph, what's wrong baby?" Tara said.

"When did you leave?" Joseph said.

"About an hour ago." Tara wasn't sure. She didn't know how long she had been gone. She just wanted to shower and relax at this point.

"We need to talk. Baby, we were going to handle all this stuff for you all." Joseph said.

"You can handle me in thirty minutes! Hey Joseph, can you let TeTe and everybody in?" Tara said as she was headed to the shower.

"Yeah, it's cold out there!" TeTe said. He had some more news for his family. "Well, everybody that bitch Paula is dead and that hoe Sherry is, too!"

"That's what I'm talking about. Hey all my brother-in-law's, what's wrong? My man JaDarrell and Joe looks like they mind is all messed up." Karen was too excited.

"Shit they are! Shit Red man, I've seen Peggy in action before but Karen and Tara are raw! Joe thinks Kezia is so nice." JaDarrell said.

"I am! Where is Pam and Paul?" Kezia laughed.

Tara had a very long day. She was ready to call it a night. She turned to her man, "Joseph, can we go to bed?"

Joseph had noticed some dried dirty looking spots on Tara. He turned to her and said, "Go take a shower baby and I'll be there in about ten minutes alright. Hey Jamel, tell all the brothers we going to have a meeting in the morning with the ladies at noon alright?"

"Karen baby, time to take a shower and lay down!" JaDarrell said.

Red hadn't felt Peggy softness in a few days. He was ready to release himself. He told Peggy to take a shower. Peggy immediately did as she was told. She was not alone no longer that two minutes. As soon as the water started feeling good to her, she found herself not being alone. Red ass got in the shower with her. The water was hitting both of their bodies. Red grabbed her and started kissing and sucking on her breast and neck going down to her navel and back up to her mouth. Peggy wanted him to make love to her badly.

They headed to the bedroom. He laid her on the bed and started kissing her inner thigh. He put his three fingers in her pussy and fucked her with his fingers. He started sucking her breast at the same time! He went back down to her inner thighs and licked and kissed her pussy. After she had come twice, he picked her up and started fucking her while he walked then laid her back on the bed. He climbed on top and started fucking her deeper.

Peggy let Red know how much she loved him. She was now about to make him feel like he had made her fell. Peggy hopped between his legs and started sucking his dick. He grabbed her hair and pushing himself in and out of her mouth, about forty-five minutes later, Red got ready to nut, and she pulled his dick out of her mouth and put his nut all over her body and she washed herself with it. Red got down on his knees and licked it all off her body like he was licking an ice cream cone!

Right down the hall was Joseph being turned on from what he was hearing. He pulled Tara close, "Tara, let me make love to you baby!"

"No, Joseph, I don't want to make love, I want to fuck tonight!" Tara said.

"Let's go into the basement so I can fuck the shit out of you and don't start crying!" Joseph said.

"Just like I said, this is a woman's world. Wait Joseph, we are gonna do something new." Tara said.

"Like what?" Joseph asked.

"Come over here and put some water in the washing machine, just a little. Let me climb on top of it. Now stand in front of me and put your dick in my pussy and I will do the rest. I got to put the machine on spin." Tara instructed.

"Oh shit Tara, damn baby that feels to motherfucking good! Oh, throw that pussy!" Joseph screamed.

"Put that shit back on spin!" Joseph said. He put her legs around his neck and started sucking all her juices out of her body. Tara came about three times and then she told him it was her turn.

Kevin knew he needed to meet with his family. He called Peggy to find their whereabouts. She let him know where they were. Kevin was there in no time. He had arrived right in time for breakfast. Kevin got updated on all things that was going on with the family. He let Karen know that he was going to be around often. His future niece or nephew needed to know him and he was not going to miss out on that.

Chapter 15

Everybody that needed to be present was sitting in the room eating their breakfast. Peggy got everyone's attention. She informed them that Sherry and Paula may no longer be around but they were just part of the problem. The root was Baby D and it was time for him to fall. She let them know what she was thinking and what she had planned. They all listened attentively.

Peggy started right in, "This is the way it's going to go down. We are gonna lock St. Louis down, we are gonna take over Mimika, Era, and Floy. Hell we are gonna take over the whole damn Northside. Hell we going to over the city!!! But we are going to make Mimika and Schulte our home base. Joseph, I need for you to call your brother Butter so we can buy from him, nothing but the good shit!"

"Peggy, what are you talking about?" Kevin wanted to know what this had to do with his daddy. He wanted the heads of those responsible for his dad laying up in that hospital bed.

Peggy ignored her brother for the time being. She had to let her family know what was on her mind. She had already discussed it with Red. She continued, "Well first we are going to get 45 keys of cocaine and 25 keys of heroin. Then we will need that black tar and take over their business. And we are going to find somebody to put the word out about our shit." Peggy seen Joseph talking on the phone, "Joseph, is that your brother?"

Joseph shook his head let her know it was his brother Butter.

"What did he say?" Peggy asked.

"Red, JaDarrell and Joe are talking price with him now." Joseph said.

"Aright, next thing we going to do is put a trace on Baby D and Eric." Peggy said.

"They are not going for that shit again, Peggy!" Tara butted in.

"Bullshit! Pam, did your make the phone call yet?" Peggy turned to Pam.

"Yeah, she down for it!" Pam said.

"What's up?" Tara needed to know what was going on.

"Tara, get my cell phone for me." Peggy instructed. She turned to her family. "Now Kezia and Pam road dog Paris is coming down here."

"Peggy, she is HIV positive!" Tara said.

"I know, we gonna clean her up and dress the shit out of her and put her on Eric. We gonna give him a death sentence. Let him think she got it going on." Peggy said.

"Where is she gonna live?" Tara was a bit concerned. She didn't know much about HIV. She just knew it was something she didn't want to be around.

"At the house on Spring Garden. I have to line somethings up. I want to make sure no one will see her being in contact with us. I don't want her connected to us at all. She will be flying out here in two days. I told her don't bring nothing. All she will have to do is locate a Western Union and all she need will be right there." Peggy didn't want anything to go wrong.

Peggy knew that Baby D was trying to be cautious of the moves he made. He was still trying to figure out what and where Joe was. She didn't know what or how much Sherry and Paula had told him. They didn't know much but she didn't know if, they had let him know that they were a huge family. Eleven girls and eight boys is what J.J. had created. Peggy didn't know if her deceased sisters had shown them pictures or shared anything about Ann with him or not. She was not taking any chances. He needed to be out the way and that was her only concern.

Butter called his brother and let him know his gift would be there in three days. Joseph said his goodbyes to his brother. Paula's face on the news had caught his attention. Someone was walking their dog and smelled a strange odor. This person had to be the nosiest person ever. He had walked around the side of the house and looked through the window. He saw Paula's dead body. He went to knock on one of the neighbor's door to ask about Paula and her recent visitors. Then he called the police. Come to find out he was a retired detective. He had surveillance around his house. His camera's only reached the sidewalk of the steps that lead to Paula's front porch. Joseph noticed Tara's pink and blue Nike Air Max.

He was outraged. He called out to Tara. He let her know what he had just seen. Tara asked him did they have her face. They both knew if they had it would be plastered on the news. They knew that the shoes were their only lead. Tara turned and looked at Joseph, "When they made that pair, she was not the first or the last to purchase some Nike air Max." She took the shoes off and said once last word to him, "And you supposed to be a lawyer!"

Red wanted to get out and enjoy the day. He went to see if his brother wanted to go shoot some pool. JaDarrell let him know he wanted to spend some time with his lady and their unborn child. Red understood so he let him be.

As JaDarrell entered the room, Karen noticed he had a concerned look on his face, "What's wrong JaDarrell?"

"I am concerned about you and the baby. There is too much going on right now. I want you to take it easy and stay off your feet." JaDarrell said as he moved close enough to rub her belly.

"Alright, baby." Karen understood what he meant.

"And in the morning, find you a doctor."

"I will, JaDarrell."

"Come here baby, don't be angry with me Karen, you are carrying my baby! And I don't want anything to go wrong with you or the baby. Let me make love to you."

"JaDarrell, it's not going to hurt the baby I hope."

He started kissing her neck and sucking her bottom lip. He laid her down on the bed and climbed on top of her and put his penis inside her pussy and she started hollering, "Darrell that shit still hurts!"

"Relax baby."

She started throwing that pussy up against his dick, "That's it baby!" he sat up in the bed, on his knees. He put her legs in his arms and started fucking the shit the out her.

"JaDarrell baby stop, it hurts!"

"Karen, who's pussy is it?"

"This yours baby?"

"And who's the man?"

"You are!"

"Now you are going to take it easy like I said."

"Yes, baby yes, please stop, I'm coming!"

"Karen cum with me sweetheart!"

He was gentle as he could be. He didn't move with force. He slowly stroked her insides.

"Karen, I meant what I said. Do you understand?"

"Yes, JaDarrell!"

"Let's take a shower."

Joseph woke up from his nap. He went down stairs looking for Tara. He walked in and saw Peggy talking on the phone.

"Well TeTe, Yane and Donuell are going to the club. Tara went, too." Peggy said.

"Tara, went where?" he asked.

"They went to the club, Joseph." Peggy informed him.

"All she snuck out while I was sleep. I'll deal with her when she get back!" Joseph stormed out of the room.

"Damn Pam and Kezia, you all glad you didn't go?" Peggy said.

"Pam, know not to pull that bullshit with me." Paul laughed.

"Shit Kezia wasn't going anywhere, were you baby?" Joe joked.

"No, Joe because I didn't want to hear your mouth all night about it." Kezia said.

Tara knows Joseph don't play that shit. Glenn and Travon told her to go check with Joseph first." Kezia said.

"I like Joseph putting Tara in her place and letting her know that he's the man!" Peggy said. "Wait until my brother-in-law see's what she has on."

"I hope it's not the dress that was hanging up there." Kezia said.

"That's the one!" Peggy said.

Everybody thought about the dress Tara had hanging on the door. It was short red and skimpy. They all said their good nights and headed to their areas that they occupied.

Tara entered the house around 5:30 in the morning. She was not sneaking but she was being quiet because she didn't want to wake anyone up.

"Oh shit, Joseph you scared me!" Tara almost jumped out of her dress.

"Not yet, what the fuck you got on?"

"A dress!"

"Let's go!"

"Joseph, I'm sorry!"

"I don't want to hear that sorry shit, you see how short that dress is, and do you hear me?"

"Yes, Joseph!"

"Go take your shower and when you get in the bed, don't touch me!" he stormed away.

"Damn, I'm in big trouble!" Tara laughed.

"Peggy, baby come here!"

"What's wrong, Red?"

"Just listen before you get mad. Betty just called my phone and said Tasha is sick in the hospital. She has been there for a week now."

"Let's go!" Peggy said.

"Are you sure?" Red asked.

"Yeah!" Peggy reassured him.

Peggy and Red left the house. Peggy had begun to say a little prayer for Tasha. She had been on her mind lately. She wanted to talk to Red about spending time with her so she could at least get to know her. She was hoping and praying it wasn't too late.

Red and Peggy entered the hospital. Peggy noticed Betty as soon as she entered the facility.

"Red, there is Betty!"

"Hey, what's wrong with her?" Red asked Betty.

Betty spoke with tears pouring down her face, "She was outside and somebody came by in a car shooting at some dude and she hit her head on the front step! They say the bullet only grazed her but I'm not sure. Blood was everywhere."

Betty told Red to go ahead to see his daughter. Red didn't really want to see her hurt. He had caused her enough pain. He vowed that he would change his ways. He was so upset with himself for not being active in her life. He prayed and told the man upstairs from this day forward he would be active in his only child's life.

Peggy figured this would be a good time to see where Betty's head was.

Peggy hugged Betty, "Everything is going to be okay. Where are you all staying?"

"We live on Lotus Avenue now."

"Girl that's drug city! When are you expecting her to be released?"

"In two more days."

Red comes out of the room and says, "Let's go Peggy, I'll check on her in a couple days."

Red didn't looked pleased. Peggy followed behind him. She didn't even get to see Tasha or tell Betty that she would see her later. Peggy asked Red was he okay.

"I'm cool. Peggy, Tasha looks just like my mother." Red said.

"Well this summer, we'll take her to see your mother!" Peggy said. She continued, "I'm going to call and have them take our house off the market. I think Betty and Tasha need not to be in that neighborhood. I know it's not safe anywhere. I believe if the word gets out on the street that Tasha is your daughter people will go after her, just to get to you."

"Peggy, is you sure?" Red asked.

"Yeah, she's your child!"

"Girl, every day I love you more and more."

"I love you too, Red."

Peggy called her brother Kevin, "Hey, how is Pop doing?"

"Fine! The doctor said he should be coming home in about four days. Joseph and Tara said that daddy is going to Joseph's other house. Glenn, Jamel, Kevin, Robert and Travon are going to stay with him there." Kevin informed her.

"That's cool! But his girlfriend can't stay there with him!" Peggy said.

"She will not even know where he's staying when he leaves the hospital. Yane and TeTe are going to stay so they can cook for him and keep eye on him."

"Does he know about Paula?" Peggy waited on Kevin's response.

"Yeah, he knows." Kevin said.

"What did he say?" Peggy was surprised.

"When asked who did it I told him Tara had taken care of it. Yane and TeTe wanted to but they moved to slow. Pop said that his daughters don't play when it comes to Jarrell."

"Fo'sho!" Peggy said.

"But he did say that no one in this family will go to the funeral and he will not pay for it!" Kevin said.

"Damn Pop put it down like that!" Peggy said.

"Hey, lets' look as some movies tonight because starting in the morning, it's all business. JaDarrell has about fifteen little cats for Joe to talk to that's going to work the south side and about twelve that's going to work on Mimika!" that was Kevin way of letting his sister know he was in and ready for the takeover she wanted to do.

Peggy ended her call with Kevin. She called Tara and let her know that everyone was pretty much down with their takeover plan. Tara reminded her of the time that Paris would arrive. She let her know that they were going to have a movie night when she got back. Tara told her to stop at the store and grab a few items so they could prepare a nice family meal. Peggy agreed and they hung up.

Chapter 16

"Peggy, wake up baby!" Red said.

"I'm up. What's wrong?" Peggy rubbed her eyes.

"Tasha is going home today. The doctor call me about twenty minutes ago." Red informed her.

"Let me take a shower and get ready." Peggy stood up and headed to the bathroom.

"Alright, I'll fix something to eat." Red was headed out the room.

"Just coffee and a boiled egg for me." Peggy placed her order for Red.

"Okay." Red said.

While in the shower, Peggy noticed her breast were getting larger. For a second she had gotten excited thinking that she might be pregnant. Then she did a mental calculation. It dawned on her that it was that time of month for her. She was brought back to reality when she heard Red yelling that her coffee and one boiled egg was ready.

Peggy didn't waste any time getting ready. She may have set a record on how fast she had gotten dressed and headed to the kitchen. She grabbed her coffee and boiled egg. She was in the car with Red headed to the hospital.

A usual forty-five minute, had easily turned into a twenty minute drive. Red was anxious to see his daughter. Peggy didn't even have a chance to drink her coffee. Had she put the coffee cup up to her mouth, she may have been wearing coffee.

Just as Red turned the corner he saw Betty and Tasha about to get into a cab. He pulled right up behind the cab. The cab began to drive away from the hospital. Red was blowing his horn like a crazy man. The cab driver pulled over and Red pulled alongside of him. Red hopped out of his truck and had a conversation with Betty. Within seconds Peggy saw Betty and Tasha exiting the cab. Red grabbed Tasha's things and paid the cab driver twenty dollars.

"Red, we live on Lotus but we are going over my friend Laura house. She said that we can stay in her basement till my mother gets another house." Betty said.

"Betty, why do you have to stay in the basement?" Peggy asked.

"Because her boyfriend don't like company." Betty replied.

"Who house is it?" Red asked.

"It's her house but her man thinks otherwise." Betty said.

"Does she have an extra bedroom?" Peggy continued with the questions.

"Yeah, but I don't mind staying in the basement!" Betty was getting a little irritated. She kept telling herself just be calm Betty.

"That's no damn friend! Where does she live?" Peggy continued.

Red had been driving and Peggy was acting like a news reporter. Both of them had distracted Betty. She didn't pay attention to the fact that Red hadn't asked her just exactly where did this friend of hers stayed. Then Betty glanced out of the window.

"Red, where are you going?" Betty asked.

"Mom, I like these big houses." Tasha said.

"Tasha, you see the big house?" Red asked.

"Yeah!" Tasha replied.

"Well, that's your new house for you and your mother." Red said as he pulled in the driveway of where he and Peggy had just moved from.

"Peggy and Red, is this for real?" Betty asked with a shocked look on her face.

"Yes, it is! But only your mother and sister can move in with you." Red said with authority.

"Red, will go this week and buy you a new car and I will carry Tasha with me tomorrow to pick out some stuff for her new house! But tonight you are going to stay at a hotel okay?" Peggy said.

Red drove three blocks from the house and turned on the main street. He pulled up to the Double Tree hotel. He told Betty all she had to do was give her name and retrieve her room key. Everything had been paid for.

"Betty, we will be here about 9:30 to pick you up." Peggy said to her, as she and her daughter exited the car.

"Peggy, yes, thank you! Now my daughter and I have a life outside of the ghetto!" Betty said.

"Betty, you have to pay the light and gas bill on your own but will keep paying the cable and the up keep of the outside ourselves okay?" Peggy said.

"Thank you." Betty said.

"And don't tell anyone that Red and I are back in St. Louis." Peggy said.

"I won't see you later." Betty said.

"Bye, Mrs. Peggy." Tasha said.

"Bye, Baby." Peggy said.

"Bye, daddy." Tasha waved.

"Tasha, that's Mr. Red." Betty said.

"No, Tasha that's your daddy!" Peggy said. She looked Tasha directly in her eyes, "You did right calling him daddy not Mr. Red."

Tasha smiled, "Bye daddy!"

"Bye baby, I'll be seeing you tomorrow. Can I have a hug and a kiss?" Red exited his truck and walked around to his daughter. He picked her up and embraced her very tightly. Peggy's heart melted.

At that very moment she wished that she and Red could share something so precious. She had never really wanted a baby so badly until that moment she saw her husband embracing his daughter. A daughter that didn't belong to her. She figured that once all the drama was over with, she and Red would be working on a child of their own. She didn't know how she would bring it up. She didn't know rather he wanted another child or not. She just wanted to give him the one thing she had never thought about giving him until she heard about Tasha.

As soon as Red kissed his daughter he headed back into his truck and his phone began to ring. Red grabbed his phone from the clip his phone was fastened to on the side of his hip. He looked down and knew what time it was when he seen Joe's name flashing across the screen. He let Joe know that he was on his way to meet him. He turned to Peggy and let her know the work had touchdown.

Peggy turned the radio on and turned to the radio to 104.9, "Oh shit Keyshia Cole new record is on. I love that song! She let that bitch know that she don't want her man! Baby, we gong clubbing so I can do the Superman."

"I heard that!" Red laughed as he watched Peggy begin to feel herself as she danced in her seat singing along with Keyshia Cole.

"Shit I want something to eat, I'm hungry!" Peggy stopped dancing long enough to get that out.

Red had something to do. Peggy would have to wait on that food or just go get it herself. He had to get busy getting rid of the work he had just found out that came in. They pulled up to where they had been recently staying. Red got out the truck. Peggy sat there feeling like Red had totally ignored that fact she was hungry. When she seen that Red was no longer in her view, she made her exited.

Peggy entered the house, "Joseph what's up, everybody here feeding their faces!"

Red ignored the comment his wife just said to his lawyer, "Alright let's get started. Joe, we have one key of heroin and key of snow. We going to give out half of each one and take it from there. I'm going to meet with JaDarrell cats today and start them on this shit tonight, alright? We will pay five hundred for the work tonight."

"Let's make some money then!" Joe said after listening to Red's plan.

Pam looked down at her text. She was informed by Kezia that Paris had arrived and she was leaving the airport. Paris was going to call them as soon as she settled in. Pam let her know that Joe had taken care of everything, so she was good to go.

Peggy looked over to her sister, "Tara, where's Joseph?"

"Upstairs, why?" Tara asked.

"Is yo ass out of the dog house?" Peggy asked.

"Yes, Peggy she's still in the dog house!" Joseph said.

"Damn Joseph, for how long." Peggy asked.

"Till I tell her she's out!" Joseph said in a matter of fact tone.

"I bet you keep your ass in the house next time!" Peggy said.

"Who side are you on sis?" Tara said.

"Lil, sis what if Baby D and them would have seen you, then what?" Peggy said.

"That's what I told her!" Joseph ranted.

"I would have killed that nigga and said fuck it!" Tara said in her matter of fact tone.

"Come with me upstairs, Tara." Joseph said.

"Oh shit Peggy, your ass got some shit started." Tara rolled her eyes and looked back at Peggy and said, "And stop laughing girl."

Tara followed behind Joseph. He was moving swiftly. She was moving slowly. She didn't want to admit but all this attention he was giving her was really turning her own.

"What Joseph?" Tara asked.

"You keep pissing me the fuck off." Joseph said.

"I don't want to hear this stuff right now!" Tara shouted.

Joseph slapped Tara in the face.

"What the fuck you hit me for?"

"I told you to act like you got some sense and you keep trying me? I'm not one of those punk ass niggas on the streets!" Joseph said through gritted teeth.

Peggy called Paris to let her know what she needed from her. She asked her if she was settled in to her place. Paris let her know things was coming along. Paris let her know that she need some more items to decorate her place. Paris let Peggy know that she was doing the Interior Designer job description for their little caper. Peggy told her she would give her a stack and she could go get what she wanted and if that wasn't enough just let her know.

Peggy got real sentimental. She asked Paris was how she feeling and was there anything that she really wanted to do. Peggy went on to tell her that all her life she wanted to leave the ghetto. She just wanted to know what it would feel like to come home to a place that wasn't infested in crime. Paris let her know that she understood, but that's all she has ever known. The ghetto was not a slum with minorities. Where she lived they were the majority. The love that was shown to one another. The sense of family that was rich on the love that they had.

Peggy saw the ghetto from a different lens. The ghetto to her was infested with poor people that did poor things. She didn't want that anymore. She wanted to live with luxurious and lavishly. She wanted to live extravagantly with no worries or hate. Paris wanted to let her know that people needed to be taught self-love. Peggy listened for a while and thought that was one conversation that wasn't needed. They would never see eye to eye on the ghetto. That was one reason Peggy was so gung-ho about putting the ghetto in her rearview.

Joe pulled up on JaDarrell to let him know about the meeting he had. They had work to get rid of and they needed some additional players to help them get rid of it.

"How did it go?" JaDarrell asked.

"Everything cool! We had thirty-five little niggas there." Joe said.

"What kind of niggas are they?" JaDarrell asked.

"They some straight up thugs. They are not afraid of shit. Four of them are from New York, I already know them. They down for their shit. I put two of them over on the south side and two of them over on the north side. And we have four that's going to be at the house on Plover." Joe said.

"Did you explain to them about Sunday? The shop will close at midnight on Saturday and open on Monday at 8 am." JaDarrell said.

"Damn Tara the meeting is almost over with and you just coming down." Joe said.

Tara looked at Joe, "I'm sure you all will put me on game."

"Yeah and Joe put Lil C over all them niggas, he will call Red or Peggy to let them know how the shit is going." JaDarrell said.

"Cool!" Tara said.

"The shipment will be tonight about 2:30." Joe said.

"Where is the drop off?" Tara asked.

"At some street called Peggy Court, first house and that's where our drop the money off. Joe can you get one of those cats to do the pickup and Jamel, Glenn and Joe are going to watch our back! Robert and J. J. will already be parked on the street, watching everything. They will get there about 9:30 tonight and Travon, will be on the next street watching everything!" Joe said.

"We got this and they will report to Joseph everything that goes on." JaDarrell said.

"Alright, then what's for dinner?" Tara asked.

"Let's go to Uncle Bill's!" JaDarrell said.

"That sounds good." Joe said.

"That's Baby D's spot!" Tara shouted.

Joseph entered the room. He knew Tara would fill him in on what he need to know. He listened for a while and found out the conversation they were having now was about food.

"Alright, then let's order and someone can go pick it up." Joe said.

"Tara, what do you want?" Joseph asked.

"Whatever you get Joseph!" Tara rolled her eyes.

"What's wrong with her?" JaDarrell whispered to Joe.

"Joseph beat her ass! I don't know if he beat her ass but he slapped the shit out of her, look at her face!" Joe whispered back.

"Stop laughing at my wife. Come here baby!" Joseph said.

"She mad because I told her Joseph was from the hood and that she couldn't run over him." Red said as he walked in the room.

"Tara, did you hear me call you?" Joseph said.

"Yeah Joseph, you have everybody laughing at me!" Tara looked towards the floor.

"Hey, Red, Lil C just called." Joe said.

"What did he say?" Red asked.

"That shit is damn good. ON the south side, blacks and whites are going crazy over that shit!" Joe said.

"Word! Put that on something!" Red said.

"He can put that on his momma! Here the call now form the north side!" Joseph said as he looked down at his phone and seen the call coming through.

"Joseph, man your brother got the bomb shit. They said the north side is loving that shit! You put half on each side." Lil C said as he talked to his longtime friend.

"Joe, took half and split it between them. Bagged that other shit up, time to make this money so we can get the hell out of St. Louis." Joseph said.

Joe turned to JaDarrell, "Did you get the guns ready for everyone?"

"Yeah, Joe!" JaDarrell answered.

"When are you gonna give them their guns?" Joe asked.

"When they are ready to put out!" JaDarrell replied.

"Alright, the store opens in the morning. Robert and Glenn, check Lil C for a few nights so we can see if he is cool or not!" Joe said.

"Alright Joe, bag as much as you can. Red can Joe help, too? Paul you ride with Travon." Joseph said. He looked down to see who was calling his phone. It was his brother Butter on the line.

"What's up? How's everything down there?" Butter asked.

"Good, real good!" Joseph said.

"Well your cake is already there." Butter said.

"Is that right! Well I'll send you a pic!" Joseph said.

"Cool." Butter shot back.

"Well your money is here. Let's get things ready for the morning. Let's go pick up and drop off. Joe, call Lil C and tell him to get his boys in check, the ones that is supposed to watch the house get them there." Joseph said to Joe once he got off the phone with his brother.

"And all the stuff they got left, sell it, the free store is closed. Red, pass out the guns now. Karen and Peggy, wait about one hour then order our food." Joseph said.

"Wait Joseph, where are you going?" Tara asked.

"We'll be back. Joe, ride with me! Did you get Lil C on the phone?" Joseph said as he brushed Tara's question off.

"Yeah." Joe said.

"Cool." Joseph shot back.

"Three months has gone by since we started moving Butter's product. The product is the best shit I ever moved. We really didn't need to step on that product at all. It's the good good shit. We got the south side on lock down and the west side, too. Man we bring in the big paper but the white folks hood is bringing in four times more than others. The north side is doing okay but they should be doing better. Joe check that shit out now." Red said to JaDarrell and Joe.

Joe called Lil C to let him know they needed to have a sit down. The money was not adding up. There was a problem and they needed to get down to the bottom of it and find out what was going on and why were they short.

"Shit, the nigga bring the shit to him about the money not adding up on the north side. We are clearing about 1.5 million a week off the north side. Every place else bring in more than that but he's checking something out and he's going to call us back. He thinks someone is stealing form him." Red said to JaDarrell as Joe talked to Lil C on the phone.

"Man in just three months we made some money." JaDarrell was trying to figure out what the issue really was. They had money and the game came with shorts.

"Hey man, how is that girl Paris doing with Eric?" Red asked JaDarrell.

"Man, the boy is in love, she fucking the shit out of him. He sucking her pussy, man the girl got a bad ass shape." JaDarrell was filling Red in on what he heard Karen and Tara talking about the other day.

"You got that right. She has a pretty face, too." Red said.

"Yeah, but she has that package, too." JaDarrell added.

Joe was waiting on Lil C to call him back. He was unaware that money was coming back short. He didn't see why would it be short. He had gotten off the phone with Joe to go check on the spots and see what was going on. He had to make sure no one was stealing from the stash.

Lil C immediately told Joe that they had to start paying niggas on Saturday when the store is closed. He found that they were not stealing although they were indirectly. They had a banking system going on. They were borrowing money and were only able to put it back of the person that was on the clock watching the money won the game.

Red turned and looked at Joe, "You mean to tell me those dumb ass niggas gambling with our money. So, if they lose our money we fucked? That some stupid shit. Man check their assess because nine months from now the hood that brought in the most money gets the big bonus. So, your little cat are taking money out of your pockets. Who are they gambling with?" Red was thinking that they were stealing and it was no way getting around it. The only explanation was stealing.

"Some dude named Quick and his brothers and some more little cats." Joe said.

"Well check this out, you are in charge right?" Red asked.

"Yeah." Joe responded.

"Well get their heads together, I'm paying these niggas five thousand a week while they are bullshitting, they are taking food out of my mouth and yours, too." Red said.

Red had to get down to the bottom line. The borrowing shit confused the fuck out of him. He couldn't believe that Joe had just said the shit to him like it made sense. He needed to talk to Lil C himself. He wanted them to know that they needed to gamble with the money they had been paid and not the money that they earned. He sat there thinking like that was some stupid shit. He looked at his brother, JaDarrell. He was wondering did the shit make sense to them.

Red decided that he needed to let Lil C know that the next time that his money was short someone would pay. He didn't want any more bloodshed but he knew he needed to send a message. He thought about telling Peggy. Then he decided against it. He knew Peggy would have clowned him and them. She probably would have gone down on the streets and told the workers. She probably would even be down there making them turn in what was loss. He quickly changed his mind about confiding in Peggy.

JaDarrell let Red know that he would have to check up with him later. Karen had a doctor's appointment that she needed to make sure she didn't miss. Today was the day she was going to get her glucose screened. Having a mother with diabetes she wanted to make sure that she didn't have gestational diabetes.

JaDarrell had looked over and seen Peggy with a little girl. Karen was confused about seeing Peggy at the doctor with a child she had no clue who was with her sister.

Peggy seen her sister Karen. She walked Tasha over to introduce her. Peggy had taken Tasha for her follow-up appointment. Betty had somethings to do and take care of. Peggy let Betty know that this would be a time that she and Tasha could bond. Betty agreed.

Joe was back on the phone with Lil C. He had found out some more information that he had to let Joe know about. Joe sat down so he can take it all in.

"What's up man?" Joe said.

"This cat named Baby D trying to throw some salt in the game talking about this his set and his hood." Lil C told Joe.

"Is he there now?" Joe asked.

"He sent the word through some cats named Rico and Boogie." Lil C continued.

"What you mean the nigga names were Rico and Boogie?" Joe asked.

"Well, I just killed them mothers fuckers to send a message and let all those nigga's know that there's a new sheriff in town." Lil C said.

"Where did you put the bodies?" Joe asked.

"They still in the car on Schulte." Lil C laughed.

"Alright, did you check your little cats?" Joe asked.

"Always, I have their heads right." Lil C said.

"Let them work and you get out the hood for a few days." Joe said.

"Fuck that, I'm cool. The ball is in that punk hands now!" Lil C.

Joe and Lil C call came to an end. He was proud that Lil C had put that work in. That message will run deep. They will think twice before gambling with someone else's money.

Peggy called Paris. She had to find out what was going on. She or no one she knew had any personal and up close contact with Paris. She didn't want Eric or Baby D to know that they were connected. Paris let her know things were working out fine. She even told Peggy that Eric had got her some clients for her fake interior designing job. Eric was impressed with how she had her home decorated. He had her decorating his mother, his aunts and just about all his family members. Peggy was impressed with what Paris had going on. She was glad things are working out. She let Paris know she would check back with her later on in the week.

Peggy called to check on Tara. Tara and Pam had went shopping in Chicago. They were driving and talking. They had so much to talk about that didn't realize that they had drove so far.

LIFE AFTER THE GHETTO

Tara was stressed to the max with Joseph being so jealous about nothing. She didn't want to leave him. No one had ever gave her so much attention. She just needed to know how to work and adjust to her independency.

Peggy, Red and JaDarrell was trying to figure out how to dismantle Baby D. They thought he was broke from the lost he had taken. JaDarrell had some information he needed to share.

"Hey check this, Karen said don't fuck with their family, but that nigga Baby D's family not in St. Louis, so what family he got behind him? Because them niggas still making money from somewhere else. Is he still buying from Butter? We need to call your brother and see if he deals with that nigga and how much that nigga buys and when." JaDarrell told his brother and his sister-in-law.

"Peggy, get the damn phone, something is wrong." Karen said to her sister.

"Yeah. What's up? Where are you? I'm on my way sis." Peggy ran on with her questions as everyone looked on to see what was going on.

"What's wrong?" Red asked.

"Tara, has been shot!" Peggy said.

"By whom?" Red asked.

"They were spotted coming home as they were getting off the highway." Peggy said.

"By who?" Red asked.

"That bitch, April." Peggy said calmly.

"Let's go." Red said.

"Who the fuck is April?" Karen asked.

"April is Baby D's cousin." Peggy said.

Peggy didn't understand why they hadn't went to the hospital. They were sitting on the Popeye's lot on West Florissant and Goodfellow. Peggy was watching Red as he drove thinking everything was okay because Tara was still talking. Pam said she thought the bullet just grazed her but she wasn't sure. She hadn't lost a lot of blood but she was bleeding. Tara said that her arm was burning.

As soon as Peggy saw Tara she was relieved. Red looked at Tara's arm. He told them it was just a graze but they still need to go to the hospital and get it checked out. They were only ten minutes away, so they headed to Barnes Hospital on Kingshighway.

Peggy told her that she was going to call Joseph and let him know. She told Tara that she was going to tell him that someone was trying to rob her and Pam. Peggy went on to tell her that's what she needed to tell the people at the hospital.

Pam started to let them know what she feels had happened before Tara had been shot, "The bitch spotted us on Grand and 70, we didn't see her at first then they shot the first shot and then we started shooting back."

"Who was with her?" Peggy asked.

"Two other girls, I didn't know them." Pam said.

They were sitting in the emergency room. When the nurse saw all the blood that Tara had on her shirt and her pants, she immediately went to her aid. She cleaned up the graze. The bullet practically went through a chunk of her arm. It sort of just broke a small portion of her skin. The nurse cleaned it up and prescribed her some pain medicine. Right before they were about to be released to leave the police arrived.

The police walked up to them to get a report. They asked for a description of the people that were trying to rob them. Peggy gave a description of Baby D. Pam sat there listening to everything Peggy had said. When the officer asked Tara was that correct, she was trying so hard not to laugh. The police officers gave Tara a card and they all went to leave.

Right as they were about to pull up Joseph had made it to the hospital. He was very upset that Tara chose to call Peggy and not him. Red had to repeat over and over again that Pam made the call. He was on ten when he got to the hospital and Tara had been released. He was trying to figure out why the fuck hadn't she called him.

Thirty minutes later they arrived home. Come in the living room everybody. "Aright listen up, the family shit is off. Whoever we can get take their ass down. Tara, Yane, Pam and I going out tonight. Kevin and Jamel can drive behind us. Paul and Travon and J. J. will go to the club with us and watch our back. The bitches are at the Loft tonight. Tara, do you know the girls faces if you see them again?" Peggy said.

"Hell yeah." Tara said.

"Joe, get on the phone with Lil C and see what the word on the street is about who those bitches are." Peggy said.

"Joseph come here. Are you mad because I have to do this? I have to point these girls out." Tara pleaded.

"I know Tara. Just make sure you come back to me." Joseph said.

"I'll be home tonight so I can suck the shit out of your dick on the dryer!" She whispered in Joseph's ear.

"That's what I'm talking about." Joseph smacked Tara on her butt.

"Joe, who was the two girls?" Peggy asked.

Some girls off the north side. They names are Joyce and Marie. The girl Marie stays on North Point right down from Goodfellow. The bitch and her boys go for bad." Joe told Peggy.

"Oh yeah! Let's take care of that whore right now!" Peggy said.

They left the house they were staying at while they had been back in town. They were on North Point in matter of seconds. They were trying to locate Marie's house. They saw a little boy standing outside. Pam asked the little boy did he know Marie. The little boy said yes. Pam asked him which house did she stay in. The little boy told her the fourth house from the corner.

Peggy put a plan in place. Two of them were going to be at the back door. They needed to make sure that no one came out that back door. When they knocked on the front door depending how the person answered they were either going to shot if they saw the person. The other choice was kick the door in and just go in shooting. Either way they were going in and kill everything that moved. No one didn't like the plan but they were not going to go against anything Peggy said.

They knocked on the door. Whomever answered the door just opened the door and walked away. They didn't ask no questions.

Peggy asked the guy as he walked away, "where is Marie?'

He didn't even finish saying she not here before Peggy shot him three times in the back of his head.

"Look who I found?" Tara said.

"She is only a baby?" Peggy asked.

"Baby! She live with these motherfuckers that has a death wish. The lil girl is trouble. Where is Joyce?" Tara asked the little girl.

"Look I'm the only one here." The little girl said. She wasn't aware of the guy that was there that they had just killed. The girl began to cry. She was only about nine years old. She didn't know how this was about to turn out.

Yane was about to kill the baby. Peggy immediately thought about Tasha. She pleaded with Yane. Yane didn't want to leave a witness. Peggy had to convince Yane to chill out. She told Yane that the child didn't have anything to do with the drama. Yane wasn't feeling letting the child leave. The child had seen their face. That child could eventually be out for vengeance. They let the child live. The little girl was able to tell them where to look for April and Joyce.

"Let's go before the police come." Yane said.

"We're going to the Spotlight you all." Peggy said.

"I think I just said that. Let's go to the Loft first. If they don't come there then we can go to the Spotlight." Tara said.

"I hope don't nobody spot these tricks when the DJ start playing Keyshia Cole or Lil Wayne." Peggy laughed.

"Girl, please stop playing." Tara said.

"Fuck that I love that Duffle Bag Boy." Peggy said.

They drove across town to the Loft. They parked and walked to the club entrance. They had made it in before eleven so there was no cover charge.

"Yane and Pam check the bathroom, me and Tara will check the V.I.P. alright. Paul and J.J. watch our back." Peggy said.

"Look at all these bitches dancing with their ass hanging out. Well, well Joyce, we met face to face." Peggy walked over to her after Tara had pointed her out.

"Who are you?" Joyce asked.

"Don't you know who you have been shooting at? It doesn't matter." Peggy said.

"Wait!" Tara yelled out.

Pam shot Joyce.

"Let's go! Pam, damn!" Peggy shook her head.

"Let's go Yane before somebody has to use the restroom. We'll get April some other time. Tara let's go, we have to take care of April on a later date." Pam said.

"Fuck that." Yane said.

"There she goes. Meet me at the motherfucking car!" Pam said as they were about to leave the club.

"Where is she?" Tara said as she looked around for April.

Peggy tilted her head in April's direction, "There she is over there hollering at some nigga."

Tara looked at Peggy, "Go ahead to the car." She walked away from Peggy and headed in April's direction.

"April!" Tara yelled out.

"What whore?" April rolled her eyes.

"Check this out." Tara sliced her throat and then her body slid down to the floor.

Tara disappeared in the darkness of the club. She moved swiftly through the dancing crowd. She was at the car right as Peggy was about to start it up.

Everybody rode home without saying a word. When they arrived home, they all took off their clothes and burned them.

"Man, Tara is my sister. But the girl needs help. Shit Yane does, too." Peggy said.

"Everybody needs to be up by 9:00 and dressed to go to church. We all need God in our life. Only he can save us from this shit." Pam said.

"Which church are we going to?" Tara asked.

"Friendly Temple on Martin Luther King and Belt. So, everybody be ready. Red we need to talk about our life. We are getting to deep into this shit. I have lived in the ghetto all my life and I know there's a better life. In the past eight months we have made so much money that we cannot keep count of." Peggy said as she took control of what Pam was trying to set up.

"What do want to do, Peggy?" Red asked.

"We can sell the house in Florida and have a house built from the ground up, how we want down south." Peggy said.

"You want to sale the house, why don't we just keep if or the summer house." Red said.

"That's cool. But next week we are going to look for some land down south so we can have our dream house built." Peggy said.

"What are we going to do about the house here?" Red asked.

"When Tasha turns 18 then we will turn it over to her and then she will come into her money." Peggy said.

"What money, Peggy?" Red said.

"Red, I know you have been putting money aside for her."

"Peggy, I was going to tell you when the time was right."

"It's cool Red."

"Peggy, when did you find out about the money?"

"Just know when I pick your brain." Peggy said in a matter of fact tone to Red.

JaDarrell began to scream, "Everybody get up!"

"What's wrong, JaDarrell?" Peggy asked.

He screamed with excitement, "Karen is in labor!"

"Here comes the pain again. What's going on, oh my God!" Karen said as she entered the room everyone was in just sitting around.

Karen didn't tell her family that she was having twins. She wanted to surprise them. She had a surprise herself. She had delivered two healthy boys. The doctor was shocked himself when he seen another baby. She had been hiding behind her brothers during the ultrasound. Karen and JaDarrell were both shocked when the doctor told them there was one more baby. Karen pushed out her last child and the afterbirth. She fell fast asleep.

"JaDarrell, you have a nice size family." The doctor said.

"Let me go tell everybody." JaDarrell went out the waiting room.

"Here comes JaDarrell. What do we have?" Peggy asked.

"We got two boys and one girl." JaDarrell said proudly.

"Man, what you say. Can we see the babies?" Red said.

"As soon as they clean them up." JaDarrell said.

"Daddy, on the phone happy as hell. Let's go see the babies, but first let's go see our sister." Kezia said.

"Karen, how you feeling?" Peggy said with a smile on her face.

"My body hurts like hell! Peggy, you laughing but I'm through fucking." Karen said with a drowsy tone.

Peggy and Pam laughed so hard till Pam pissed on herself. Here come all your brothers.

"Hey sis, how are you feeling?" Paul asked.

"Don't ask and Pam shut up!" Karen said.

The girls were all excited. Those were going to be some spoiled little babies. Peggy was really ready to give Red a baby. Within a few days, Karen and the babies were released. It was a good thing that they were all still in the house together. Karen and JaDarrell had more than enough help. Peggy was feeding her niece when she got a call from her friend from the clinic. Her friend was out on a smoke break and let her know that she had the news she had been waiting on.

Peggy walked into the room to put her niece in the bassinet. She was looking for Tara and Pam. They were in the basement smoking a blunt.

"I hear Eric is looking for Paris. He got that gift she gave him!" Peggy laughed.

Tara looked at Peggy, "How the fuck he just going to put that on Paris. He act like she the only one he been fucking."

Peggy laughed, "I guess he going after the last one. It doesn't matter. He got it and it ain't shit he or we can do about it now!"

"Peggy, you want us to kill this nigga?" Pam asked.

"No, let him have a slow death. Everybody come into the living room so we can talk. JaDarrell you can fill Karen in on what we are talking about. Okay, we all here now, we made a lot of money. We have St. Louis on lockdown all the way down. And the crew has put their life on the line for us the last nineteen months!" Peggy said.

"So, what are you saying, Peggy?" Pam asked.

"What I'm saying is for the next two or three months, all the money we make will be for the crew so they can have something to fall back on. It is time to start thinking ahead. Red and I are flying out in the morning to check on some land so we can have our dream house built. I think everybody should do something because nothing last forever." Peggy said.

"I'm with you, sis." Kezia said.

"Me, too!" Pam said.

"Man, who would ever have thought that teaming up with our sister would have made us this rich and put us on top of the world." Paul said.

"Well since we are talking, Paul and I have been talking to this company that is going to build our home." Pam said.

Everyone sat and discuss their plans for the money they had earned. Everyone had decided St. Louis would always be home but they were going to a new place and try new things. They were talking about land, having houses built and even starting some sort of business. Their conversation was brought to an end when Peggy phone rang.

Peggy was listening to her caller and tears began to roll down her eyes. The tears disappeared and Peggy was now frowning. She went from crying to being very angry. She was listening attentively as her family looked on. They couldn't wait until she ended that call they needed to know who was on the phone and who had her feeling bad. Peggy asked her caller what she wanted to do. Then she said no problem and ended the call.

Peggy let her family know that it was one thing they needed to do before they all departed. They were going to Paris house and wait on Eric to get there. Him dying a slow death was not going to happen. Peggy was feeling some sort of way. Paris having that package didn't sit well with Peggy. She despised that disease. She didn't know when Paris would close her eyes forever but she wanted her to enjoy the little life she had left. Peggy didn't want them to know how Paris had her feeling. Paris really had the upper hand. She could have asked Peggy for everything she owned and Peggy would have given it to her. Peggy just wanted Paris to be happy.

Peggy and her sisters were at Paris's home. They were waiting on their victim. Paris let them know that he was going to meet her there. Peggy told Paris to turn off all the lights. They were going to wait in the bedroom.

"Hey, Peggy I think this is a setup!" Joe said.

"Why do you think that?" Peggy asked.

"Something just doesn't feel right." Joe said.

"Well what do you want to do, Joe?" Peggy asked.

"Let me tell Red and JaDarrell to be posted by the back door. Go unlock the back door so they can get it?" Joe said.

Peggy went to unlock the back door. She checked all the rooms to see where everyone was. She laughed when she saw Paris sitting on the toilet as though she was using it. She sent everyone a message to let them know that Paris was in the bathroom. Before Peggy went into the room with Joe, she went back to the bathroom. She told Peggy just fall into the bathtub as soon as she heard the first gun shot.

Tara was sitting outside. Peggy was holding her phone waiting on the text message to come through. She had already looked at a phone four times. When she took her final look, she looked over at Joe, "It's about six of them and they are on their way in."

"Paris, baby do you have on clothes. I have my boys with me. I want you to meet Baby Boom and Wayne."

Paris was looking abnormal. She wondered why he would bring people around her that she hadn't met before. She told them hello but she began to get butterflies.

Eric could hear a phone vibrating. He went looking for the vibration. Tara had just texted Peggy to let her know that their brother Robert was on his way in. Peggy wanted to text her back but Eric was in her face. Good thing Joe came from the shadows and his strapped had a silencer. Eric fell to the ground before he even knew what happened.

Robert caught two bullets coming through the door. Wayne ended his life before he even had two feet in the door. Wayne and

Boom were too busy looking at Robert that never seen Joe and Peggy coming. Peggy walked over and hugged Paris.

"Thank you and I appreciate all that you have done for me." Peggy thanked Paris. "Joe, let's get my brother to the car. Damn Robert baby hold on, get him to the car, we will meet you at the hospital, go Jamel! I don't believe this shit, I hope my brother is not gone!" Peggy began to cry.

Robert had died before they even made it to the hospital. They pulled up to the emergency entrance. One of Joe's friends were working security. Joe walked over to the security desk and spoke to his friend. The friend called the emergency room doctor out the car. The doctor and nurses were so busy getting Robert out the car they didn't ask any questions. Everyone that stood around the car were wearing frowns. Within ten minutes the doctor announced Robert as dead.

The drive back home was very long. All you heard was crying.

"Come on baby, JaDarrell you go tell Karen." Peggy said.

"What's going on baby?" Karen said as she seen everyone coming through the door.

"Robert got killed!" JaDarrell said as tears rolled down his face.

"Joseph, did you call Jarrell?" Tara asked wondering had he called her dad like she had asked.

"I told him! He wants the body to be taken to Mississippi." Joseph said.

Two days later, Red and Joseph went to Mississippi to make arrangements for the family. Red was also checking on the ground where they were going to build their new house. Peggy let Red know that she had a referral that he could contact once he got there. After he and Joseph had taken care of the funeral arrangements Red went to see the realtor who was going to assist with helping them find their future home.

Joseph put the address the realtor in his GPS. They found the office to the real estate agency with no problem. Joseph parked the car and only Red went in to speak with the agent. As soon as he walked through the door the agent was there to greet him.

"Hell Mr. Strong, how are you doing?" the agent asked.

"Fine, sir." Red responded.

"So, Mr. Strong you want eight bedroom, four bathrooms, an indoor and outdoor pool. Along with a fireplace in every bedroom!" the agent was making sure that the request was correct.

Red let him know that information was correct. He had to continue with his list of wants. Red said to the realtor, "A big fish tank built in the wall and a theatre built on the lower level that seats thirty people and a game room is also amenities that I need. My wife will get back with you about everything else."

"Okay." The realtor felt he had enough to get started.

LIFE AFTER THE GHETTO

Five days later, everybody was at the funeral and the sisters were taking it very hard.

"As of today, these bitches in St. Louis will feel us. We are going to close down Mimika for good." Peggy said as they were about to leave the funeral and head back home.

Peggy got a call from a longtime friend. The friend let her know that they had a lead on Baby D's and his crew whereabouts. She was happy because she had to revenge her brother, Robert's death. The friend had information on where Baby D's mother had resided.

Peggy, Pam, Kezia and Tara were looking for the house where his mother lived. They were riding up and down Dave Drive. They were trying to make sure Baby B was not about to come out. They were also trying to check to see if he had anyone watching his mom's house and trying to keep her safe. When they notice everything was peaceful they parked the car. Peggy had the address memorized. Peggy walked right up to the front door with her sisters in tow.

Peggy turned to them and said, "All right now listen, let's get all the information we can get and when we leave this motherfucker, everybody here will be sleep for good."

"But no kids, Peggy." Kezia said.

"Fuck that, everybody in this bitch going to sleep alright! It's your call!" Tara said.

Peggy looked back at Tara and smiled.

They knocked on the door. The person on the other side of the door looked out the peep hole but couldn't make out the images.

"Yes, who are you?" his mother asked.

"Hi, my name is Vee and I'm here to see Baby D." Tara said.

"Baby D, is not here." His mother said.

"I know. He wanted me to wait for him until he gets here." Peggy lied.

"Alright, come on in." his mother opened the door.

"Thank you. I got to get something out of my car. I'll be right back." Peggy said.

"Ok, baby." His mother said.

"Come on you all. Pam go to the left and Kezia you go to the right. Tara, you come with me." Peggy said.

When they got inside the house, Tara could feel something wasn't right. She told Peggy that something wasn't right about this. As Pam and Kezia entered the house they both sensed something wasn't right themselves with the old lady. Getting into the house was way too easy. Because when she let Peggy in, she left herself. His mother never came back to check on her or anything. So, they started looking around the house for her.

"Baby D got all this money and let his mother live like this." Peggy said.

As they were searching the house, looking for clues that could lead them to Baby D, they smelled something that was very foul. As they entered into the dining room there sat Baby D's mother eating some food that looked like it was cooked over two weeks old. It smelled worse than day old cabbage that was left out all night. The chicken was so dried out that it looked like she had it for over a year. Pam walked over to the lady and put her arm around her. Then she asked her why was she eating that nasty food. And she told her that the food would make here sick. She looked at everyone and told them that it was all she had. Kezia sat down to ask her where was here son. She said that he doesn't come by much. Pam asked her what was her name and she told her Mrs. Connect.

"Mrs. C when was the last time you saw Baby D?" Pam asked.

His mother stopped eating for a second. It was long enough to them it had been about three months ago that he had passed through.

"Well, Mrs. C, we are going to buy you some food for this house and make sure you get everything you need." Pam said to her letting her know they would be right back.

As they got outside and looked at each other, Peggy told them something is not right. She needs some answers.

As Peggy eased her way back into the house, she heard Mrs. C on the phone with Baby D telling him everything that went down and that they bought the whole thing. When she turned around and saw Peggy's face she used the chair to hold herself up. As she started shitting all over herself, Peggy over took her and hung up the phone.

"Mrs. Connect, did you think I bought that bullshit you were feeding my sisters? For one when you said you name was Mrs. Connect I knew it was a setup. See I'm from the streets and I know what connect means. You the one to set the trap for us, but I'm not going to hurt you because I know that you were trying to protect you son like all mothers do." Peggy said.

Tara walked in to Baby D's mother house. She overheard Peggy talking to the woman. She couldn't believe the woman and lied. Tara was not going to let her get away with that. Tara walked in and looked at the lady and said connect this bitch. She shot her twice in the head and looked at Peggy, "Let's get the fuck out of here." Tara said and turned to walk away.

They hopped in Kezia car and pulled off. Two days later they found Mrs. C's body. It was found by her son Percy who had come home from school for a visit. When Percy saw his mother lying on the floor with two holes in her head, he damn near lost his mind. When the word got out about Baby D's mother, his boys started helping Baby D get things ready for his mother's resting place.

Baby D and his brother Percy and their cousin April cried their eyes out. They climbed up in their mother's bed and just cried themselves to sleep. The next day when Baby D had gotten up, he woke April up and they went downstairs to talk about how they were going to put their mother away. As April was calling R. L. Jones to make that arrangements, Baby D looked at her and told her that he was out of the drug game.

April looked at him like he was crazy. "You mean you just going to let them get away with killing our mother?" she said.

"April, once we have mom funeral, everybody will be getting ready to know that we are sister and brother. So niggas that you have the ups on is gonna want some answers." Baby D said.

"Where do we go from here?" April asked.

Percy sat on the steps and listened to his brother and sister crying.

April looked at Baby D and said, "You know that bitch Peggy Clark did this shit! She has to pay for what she has done to our mother!"

While they were sitting down talking. Percy eased his way in the guest room and called the police and told them who killed his mother and the person's name.

Four days later they were at their mother's funeral trying hard to be strong for each other. When they got home April asked Baby D what they are going to do. Percy told them what he heard they say and what he did. Baby D and April knew it was time to go. April told them they got money, more than they could ever spend. She told both her brothers it was time to leave.

They emptied out the safe and hopped into three different cars and headed out. Percy put a plan together for them. They drove to East St. Louis, sold their cars and took the train to

Kentucky. From there they are to take a plane to Utah to start all over again.

In the meanwhile Peggy's face was shown on the TV everywhere for the murder of Mrs. Bee Davis.

When they saw that all over the news, Red and everybody damn near shit on themselves.

Red turned and started yelling, "Peggy, what the fuck are they talking about?"

Before Peggy could say anything Tara said, "Peggy didn't do it. I did it."

Everybody turned around and looked at Tara. Joseph looked at his wife and damn near fell out.

Pam started talking. She wanted to know how the fuck did they come out with Peggy's name. Joseph got himself together and told them to close all shops down. Kevin asked JaDarrell how much more work do they have on the streets and JaDarrell said about three million dollars' worth. Before Kevin could say anything Peggy told them just let the work keep making the money on the street. When they sellout, which will be about two weeks or less, close shop and send everybody on a trip till things cool off!

Peggy turned to Joseph and said, "So, that way the police cannot link them to us. Joseph, find me the best damn lawyer money can buy."

Joseph said to Peggy, "They think O.J. had the dream team. Motherfucker has not seen anything."

Joseph got started first thing in the morning. Peggy seen Joseph working the telephone trying to help her. He had called seven people while she was standing there.

When he ended the last call she spoke, "Joseph when you get the lawyers together and build your case, I will turn myself in. Kevin, Glenn, Joe and Paul will keep their eyes on the crew. When they meet up in Las Vegas, Jamel and Travon will get with TeTe and Yane and make sure that their money is right and then give all them their money. The way I see it, every one of them should have at least seven million for themselves. But the leader should have 10 million. Red and I are leaving tonight. Tara and Kezia will know how to get in touch with me. I'll leave everything that Tara and Kezia need to reach me." Peggy hoped that Joseph understood her what she was rambling on about everything that had bombarded her mind.

"Peggy your phone is ringing. Joseph informed her.

"Hello." Peggy said.

"Peggy, can you talk?"

"Who is this?"

"Gator."

"What's up boy? How are you doing?"

"Okay!"

Gator was that crack head that's crazy about Peggy. He always had the 411 for Peggy.

"Listen Peggy, the police is everywhere asking about you. Peggy, get the hell out of St. Louis now."

Gator has always looked out for Peggy. When he had lost his job for sucking on that glass dick and lost everything, Peggy helped him out with a place to live and with a little money every month so he can take care of his kids.

Peggy thanked Gator. She let him know that she was going to slide something to him. He told her keep in touch and they ended their conversation.

Peggy went to talk to Red. She let him know that she needed to leave. They just needed to leave until they reached their destination. As they were about to get on the highway she seen Baby D picture up on a billboard as missing. They had left just in time. The police raided their known place of residence. Betty just had too much information and was not solid. She didn't even appreciate the fact Peggy had given her and her child a place to stay. She told the police where they could find Peggy.

Karen, JaDarrell, Tara and Joseph had not left the house yet. They were trying to get things together. Joseph was trying to work on Peggy's case right when the police kicked the door down. No one moved. They were too scared to make a move. Peggy had been labeled as arm and dangerous. They didn't want to take any chances.

When the officers seemed too had settled down, Joseph let them know that he was a lawyer. He asked who or what they were looking for. One officer stepped up and informed him that they were looking for Peggy Carter.

When they came in the living room he told them that he was the lawyers ready and what they were looking for in the case.

When all the officers left, Tara had questions for Joseph. She knew Peggy wanted to turn herself in. Tara didn't think that would be her best choice. Tara needed to know would Peggy be able to make a bond once she turned herself in. Joseph let her know he was not sure. It would all be on how the district attorney was prosecuting the case. He let her know that he had six other lawyers that were willing to help him and Peggy out. Joseph told Tara that she needed to call Peggy and tell her to be there in a week to turn herself in.

That week flew by. Peggy was back in town. She was ready to turn herself in. She was sitting in her hotel room when she called Gator. Peggy needed Gator to work the streets and find out everything he could. He was pleased with the stack she dropped on him the last time. She ended her call letting him know she would look out for him.

Joseph called Peggy to let her know that he had made the call. She could go ahead and get ready to turn herself in.

Tara asked, "How strong of a case do they have?"

Joseph answered, "I'm not really sure."

Everyone went to the hotel to see Peggy. She wanted to come to the house but Joseph let her know that was not a good idea. He believed that they were being watched. Everyone walked into the hotel room with their eyes filled with tears.

Everybody hugged and kissed and cried. Then Red turned to Joseph and asked him what the deal is with the case. After Joseph told them what he found out, Joe came in and told them what the word on the street was. That someone called the police and gave Peggy's name and that the police wanted to talk to her about Spring Garden.

"Well In the morning we will find out what they got. Let's eat dinner and get ready for the morning." Peggy said.

"Peggy, the lawyers will meet us at the jail house at 9 am. Peggy grabbed her phone and went to the bathroom. When she closed the door she called Gator. When he answered, Peggy told him she needed his help. Without thinking Gator told her anytime anyplace. Gator knew she meant to work on the street and find out everything he could.

The next morning everybody was up and ready. They arrived at that jail house ten minutes early. The other attorney was waiting there to meet Peggy. Some body at the jail called the newsroom and let them know that Peggy was turning herself in. All the news channels were there. They were trying to talk to Peggy while her lawyers walked into the jail house. They put Peggy in a room and tried to shut the door before all seven attorneys walked in to talk to their client.

She was with her lawyers for about three hours and then walked in the pigs. Everyone said their names starting with Peggy's then her attorneys introduced themselves. Mr. Fox, Mr. Love, Mr. Jones, Mr. Keys, Mr. Glade, Mrs. Grabber and Mrs. Black. Then there was Officer Biden and Officer Snow.

Just as Peggy turned around, Officer Card came in and read Peggy her rights for the murder of Mrs. Bee Davis. Peggy got up and put her hands behind her back for them to put the cuffs on her with her attorneys by her side. Mr. Love asked them to show the evidence that they had and Officer Snow told them they have a person who can identify her.

As they took Peggy away, someone in the jail house fired two shots and then ran out. The police were all over the place but the shooter was a goner. Everybody raced over to Peggy to see what they could do to help her.

Pam looked up and started screaming. Pam fell to her knees and looking up to the sky, "God please bring her back."

Red couldn't take anymore. He had vengeance in his thoughts. He ran out of the police station. The police where all over the building. Everyone that was in the police station was instructed to lay down on the floor. EMT was at the police station fast. When they heard someone had been shot at the police station, they automatically thought it was an officer.

Red was driving and crying. He had no idea of where he was going. All he knew was that his wife had been shot. He had images of Peggy on replay in his thoughts. He constantly heard her saying, "Put me away nice."

Red was not trying to hear that. He could not imagine his life without Peggy. He needed to do something. He just didn't know what to do. He ignored his thoughts as he seen Peggy's name come across the screen of his cell phone...

RENITA TOWNS

Made in the USA
Monee, IL
15 November 2023